PUFFIN CANADA

CAMP X

Eric Walters is an elementary school teacher who began writing as a way to encourage his students to become more enthusiastic about their own creative writing. He is the author of a number of acclaimed and bestselling novels for children, including *Stand Your Ground,* which was a regional winner of the Silver Birch Award, *STARS, Trapped in Ice,* which was shortlisted for the Ruth Schwartz Award and the Silver Birch Award, *The Hydrofoil Mystery* and *Royal Ransom*. Eric Walters lives in Mississauga, Ontario, with his wife and their three children.

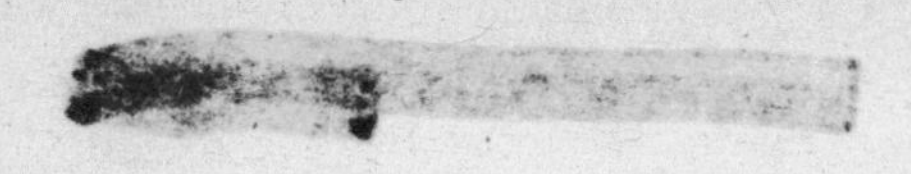

Also by Eric Walters from Penguin Canada and Puffin Canada

*The Bully Boys*
*The Hydrofoil Mystery*
*Trapped In Ice*
*Royal Ransom*

Other books by Eric Walters

*Tiger Town*
*Ricky*
*Road Trip*
*Northern Exposures*
*Long Shot*
*Tiger in Trouble*
*Hoop Crazy*
*Rebound*
*Full Court Press*
*Caged Eagles*
*The Money Pit Mystery*
*Three-on-Three*
*Visions*
*Tiger by the Tail*
*War of the Eagles*
*Stranded*
*Diamonds in the Rough*
*STARS*
*Stand Your Ground*

# CAMP X

ERIC WALTERS

PUFFIN
CANADA

PUFFIN CANADA
Published by the Penguin Group
Penguin Books, a division of Pearson Canada, 10 Alcorn Avenue, Toronto, Ontario, Canada M4V 3B2
Penguin Books Ltd, 80 Strand, London WC2R 0RL, England
Penguin Putnam Inc., 375 Hudson Street, New York, New York 10014, U.S.A.
Penguin Books Australia Ltd, 250 Camberwell Road, Camberwell, Victoria 3124, Australia
Penguin Books India (P) Ltd, 11, Community Centre, Panchsheel Park, New Delhi – 110 017, India
Penguin Books (NZ) Ltd, cnr Rosedale and Airborne Roads, Albany, Auckland 1310, New Zealand
Penguin Books (South Africa) (Pty) Ltd, 24 Sturdee Avenue, Rosebank 2196, South Africa

Penguin Books Ltd, Registered Offices: 80 Strand, London WC2R 0RL, England

First published in Viking by Penguin Books Canada Limited, 2002
Published in Puffin Canada by Penguin Books, a division of Pearson Canada, 2003

10 9 8 7 6 5 4 3 2 1



*Publisher's note: This book is a work of fiction. Names, characters, places and incidents either are the product of the author's imagination or are used fictitiously, and any resemblance to actual persons living or dead, events, or locales is entirely coincidental.*

Manufactured in Canada.

NATIONAL LIBRARY OF CANADA CATALOGUING IN PUBLICATION DATA

Walters, Eric, 1957–
Camp X / Eric Walters.

ISBN 0-14-131328-5

1. Great Britain. Special Operations Executive. Special Training School 103 (Whitby, Ont.)—Fiction. 2. World War, 1939–1945—Secret service—Great Britain—Fiction. 3. World War, 1939–1945—Secret service—Canada—Fiction. 4. World War, 1939–1945—Military intelligence—Canada—Fiction. I. Title.

PS8595.A598C36 2003 C813'.6 C2002-904472-3
PZ7



Visit Penguin Books' website at **www.penguin.ca**

*This book is dedicated to the memory of Sir William Stephenson and the men and women who served and trained at Camp X. These very ordinary people came together to do something extremely extraordinary—they helped to save the world.*

# CHAPTER ONE

A TWIG SNAPPED UNDER my feet and I froze at the sound. How far had the noise travelled? Had I been heard? My heart raced and I held my breath, listening, listening. There was nothing but the sound of crickets softly chirping in the twilight.

Slowly I turned my head, scanning the surroundings, looking, trying to spot any movement in the trees and bushes on all sides. Nothing. There was nothing. Or at least nothing that I could see.

I pulled my weapon in closer to my chest, almost as if it were some sort of shield or screen that could protect me from unseen eyes or weapons—eyes that I knew were out there, looking for me, the same way I was looking for them.

Slowly I started moving again, trying to stay in the shadows cast by the setting sun. Another twenty minutes and it would be down and I'd be safe, or at least safer, from prying eyes. Of course, not being seen meant that I couldn't see either. Places where I could hide were also places where my enemy could stand undetected until I walked right up and they could aim weapons at me and—I stopped dead in my tracks.

Just off to the side I heard a noise. Or thought I heard a noise. Maybe it was nothing. Maybe it was just my imagination, or even a rabbit or a—the noise came again. This time it was louder and clearer. It was the sound of feet moving over gravel. I knew there was a path just a couple of dozen yards off to that side—I'd crossed over it and then deliberately travelled parallel to it through the cover of the forest. Whoever it was, he was coming down the path.

I bent over so I couldn't be seen above the bushes. I started to angle toward the path, slowly and deliberately, hardly lifting my feet, keeping under cover and in the shadows. He was still coming—I could hear him—but he didn't know I was there. Just up ahead I could see a gap in the trees . . . a place where I'd be able to see the path, and anybody coming down it. Softly I dropped to my knees behind a fallen tree. I pulled up my rifle and set it down on the trunk of the log, using it to steady my shaking hands. Here I'd wait for him to cross into my sights, and then . . .

Silently I took a deep breath in through my mouth, holding it in my lungs for a few seconds before exhaling through my nose. I had to control my breath, my heart and my shaking hands. I might only have one chance, and if I failed to kill him, then his gun would be trained on me. It was me or him. Me or him. A shiver went through my entire body.

I turned my head ever so slightly, listening for the sound of his footsteps. Why couldn't I hear anything? Had he stopped or turned around? Even worse, had he turned off the path? Had he heard me moving through the trees the way I'd heard him? And if he had, was he at this very moment coming up behind me and . . . I felt the hairs on the back of my neck stand up on end as I slowly moved my head to look behind me. Nothing. At least nothing that I could see.

I was overcome by a rush of fear. I had to get out of there . . . retreat farther into the trees . . . take cover in the darkness where I couldn't be found. I started to rise to my feet when—there it was again—the sound of feet against gravel. He was still coming.

I lowered myself back down until I was completely hidden by the fallen tree. The rifle rested against the trunk and I pressed my face against it, one eye closed, the other sighting down the barrel of my weapon. It was only going to be a matter of seconds before he walked right past this spot and—there he was! A Nazi, my sworn enemy. A small smile crept onto my face. In a split second there'd be one fewer Nazi in the world to battle the forces of freedom.

He was moving down the path slowly. I could tell by the way he was walking that he was trying to muffle the sound of his footfalls. He held his weapon out before him, looking first left and then right, scanning the forest. He was looking for me. Little did he know just how soon he was going to find me, and that he was going to pay for that privilege with his life.

He came forward, closer and closer, still partially hidden by the trees. I had to wait until he came completely into the opening, where there was no place for him to hide. In the dim light I couldn't see his face. Maybe that was better. I didn't want to be haunted by the eyes of another dead man. He crept forward . . . another few feet before he'd be square in my sights . . . wait . . . wait . . . wait . . . I squeezed the trigger and—

"BANG!" I yelled. "I got ya!"

"You missed me!" he screamed back.

"What do you mean I missed you?" I demanded as I jumped to my feet. "You were only twenty feet away and—"

"Bang, bang, bang! I got *you!*" he yelled.

"How could you get me when you're already dead!"

"I wasn't dead . . . I was just wounded! You only winged me!"

"You're dead! Look how close I am!" I yelled.

"You were close, but you're a bad shot. All Nazis are bad shots!"

"I'm not a Nazi! You're the Nazi!" I screamed. "I was the Nazi the last time!"

"You're always the Nazi, George."

"That's not fair!"

"I'm the big brother so I get to decide what I am, and if you don't like it I'm not playing!"

"Come on, Jack, couldn't I please be the—?"

"Nope," he said, cutting me off. "Either you're the Nazi or I'm not going to play war with you any more. I'm too old for this anyway. If I was just a few months older I'd be fighting them for real!"

"A few months? You're only fourteen," I protested.

"Yeah, well, some sixteen-year-olds are fighting in the war," he argued.

"You're still twenty months away from being sixteen. And even if you were sixteen there's no way Mom would let you join up."

"But Dad might."

"I don't think so," I said.

"And maybe he and I could be in the same platoon and fight the Nazis together," my brother continued.

"You're dreaming if you think that either one of them is going to—"

"Then I'll join the French Foreign Legion, or get some false papers and join the British Army or something!"

I knew there was no point in arguing with him. He wanted to fight the Nazis . . . but who didn't?

War was raging across Europe and Asia and Africa. It was all happening pretty far away from Canada but we read about it in the newspapers, and there were the reports on the radio, and the Pathe newsreels we saw at the movies. And of course there were the letters from our father, coming from somewhere in Africa where he was stationed, fighting against the Nazi menace, helping to free the world.

I looked around. Night was closing in quickly and I wasn't exactly sure where we were.

"Jack . . . are we lost?" I asked hesitantly.

"Of course not. Don't *you* know where we are?"

"Well . . . I think that the highway is sort of that way," I said, pointing off into the distance.

"Wrong," he said, shaking his head. Even the fading light couldn't disguise the look of disgust on his face. "That way," he said, pointing off to the side.

"Are you sure?"

"Of course I'm sure. Turn around."

I looked over my shoulder. There was a glow in the darkening sky.

"You know what that is, don't you?" he asked.

I nodded my head. It was the security lights at the plant. The plant was part of D.I.L.—Defence Industries Limited. It was a gigantic munitions factory and the reason we'd moved to Whitby, Ontario. Two months ago, at the end of the school year we'd left behind our farm—it was too hard to work it with Dad gone—and moved here so Mom could work at the factory.

"I guess we should be heading home," I said.

"What's wrong . . . is little Georgie afraid of the dark?"

"I'm not afraid of the dark," I protested.

"You want to fight the Nazis and you're afraid of the dark," he chided me. "You know they don't stop fighting when it gets dark!"

"Shut up, Jack . . . or else!"

"Or else what?"

"Or else . . . or else I'll tell Mom."

"You're such a baby, running to your mommy. You act more like a two-year-old than a twelve-year-old."

"I'm not a twelve-year-old . . . yet." My birthday was in two weeks.

"Don't give me a hard time or you may not make it to your birthday." He paused. "Come on."

"Home is the other way!" I said, grabbing him by the arm as he started to walk away.

"Don't worry, Georgie, I'll protect you from any big bad bunny rabbits that might jump out and try to hurt you."

"I'm not afraid of any animal. I just think we should get home. What if Mom calls on her break and we're not there?" I asked.

She was on the swing shift today, from four in the afternoon until midnight, and my brother was "watching" me. She was on three different shifts: two weeks on days, two weeks on the evening swing shift and then two weeks working from midnight until eight in the morning. Once September came, at least the day shift wouldn't be so bad because we'd be in school.

"What time is it?" my brother asked.

I tried to look at my watch. There wasn't enough light to see it clearly, but it had to be close to nine. Mom had her dinner break between seven-forty-five and eight-fifteen, and if she had tried to call us she wouldn't have got an answer. She'd be calling back on her next break . . . that was just before ten.

"I'm not sure. It has to be nine . . . maybe even nine-ten," I said, deliberately making it sound later so we could leave. "You'll be in big trouble if she calls and we're not back."

"All right, let's go that way," he said, pointing in the direction he'd originally proposed.

"But we have to get home."

"We are going home. A shortcut."

"How can heading in the wrong direction be a shortcut?" I asked.

"Trust me," he said, and he started walking.

Helplessly I trailed behind him. "How can this be faster?"

"It will be. Instead of cutting through the bush we're going to take a straight line," Jack explained.

"What straight line?"

"That one," he said, pointing up ahead.

I didn't see anything, just the dark outline of a hill or a bank of some kind.

"Do you know what that is?" he asked.

I shook my head.

"The railroad tracks. We'll climb up the embankment and walk along the tracks until we hit a road, and then we'll follow the road."

"Wouldn't it be faster to just go back the way we came?" I asked.

"Too dark."

"Are *you* afraid of the dark?" I chided him.

"Nope. You go that way if you want. I'll meet you at home. We could make it like a race and see who gets there first, okay?"

I knew what he was doing. I also knew he was doing it well.

"I'll go with you," I said quietly.

Even in the thin light I could see a smug look creep over his face.

I trailed behind Jack. The ground was pretty rough and we had to move around dense bush and trees. Up ahead the railroad embankment loomed larger and larger until finally we stood right before it.

It was a massive pile of dirt and gravel and stones and cinders that had to be at least twenty feet high. Jack started up the slope. I hesitated at the bottom.

"What if a train comes?" I asked.

"Get out of its way," he called over his shoulder as he kept on climbing. "Don't worry, we're only going to take it until we find a road."

I looked along the embankment as far as I could see in the limited light. There was no road visible to the right. I turned the other way and—

"Jack! I see a road!"

He stopped and turned around. "You do? Where?"

"Just down that way," I said, pointing toward it.

There was a pause. "I don't see . . . wait, I think I do see something. It looks like it goes *under* the tracks."

He scrambled down the slope, rocks and gravel showering down in front of him. We walked along the base of the steep bank toward the road. As we closed in I could see that it was more of a dirt trail. Maybe it didn't lead anywhere.

We stopped and looked. There was an underpass. The dirt track led right to a culvert that ran beneath the tracks. It was made of curved metal. It wasn't big . . . maybe large enough for a tractor or one car to pass through, but not much more.

"Which way do we go?"

"The highway is that way," Jack said, pointing away from the culvert.

"Good, then let's—"

"But I think we should go the other way," he said cutting me off. "Aren't you curious to know what's in that direction?"

"Well . . ."

"Don't be scared."

"I'm *not* scared!"

"Then come on," he said.

Before I could say another word he started walking toward the culvert, and I scrambled after him.

Inside it was even darker, and there was a damp mustiness. I caught up to Jack as he stopped in the very middle of the tunnel.

"There's really an echo in here," he said.

"There is," I agreed, and my voice bounced back at me.

I practically jumped into the air when Jack yelled "Heeellllloooo!" and his voice boomed back a second time. "ECCCHHHO!" he screamed, and then he laughed as his voice bounced around us.

"Why don't you try saying some—?"

He stopped mid sentence as we both heard the same thing—an engine. There was a car or a tractor coming! I turned to say something just as the whole end of the tunnel exploded in light! There was a car coming straight for us!

"Come on!" Jack yelled, and we started running in the other direction.

"Identify yourself!" yelled out a voice.

The way out was blocked by two men—men carrying rifles—illuminated in the lights of the car closing in from behind. Their guns were trained on us!

"Drop your weapons or we'll shoot!" one of them bellowed.

# CHAPTER TWO

"DROP YOUR GUNS!" ONE of the men screamed.

"Our guns . . . they're just toys," I stammered. "Just toys!"

"Now!" screamed the second man.

I dropped my toy rifle to the ground, as did Jack. I looked at my brother and his face reflected the terror I was feeling. Who were these men and what did they want with us?

The two men rushed forward, and when I turned to run I was smashed from behind. The air rushed out of my lungs as I landed heavily on the ground and my face dug into the dirt.

"They're just kids," a voice called out.

Suddenly I was pulled to my feet by powerful hands. One man was holding on to the back of my shirt, practically hanging me from the scruff of my neck, while a second held onto Jack. I was helpless and terrified. My mind was numb and I was fighting hard not to cry. Two more soldiers stood right in front of us, their rifles at the ready.

"What are you kids doing here?" the one soldier demanded angrily.

"We were just—"

"This is a restricted area!" he yelled, cutting off my brother. "Didn't you see the signs?"

"Signs? We didn't see any—"

"They say 'Restricted Area—Keep Out.' They're posted all along the road."

"We didn't come along the road! We came in through . . . through the field . . . over there," Jack stammered, pointing back the way we'd come.

"And why were you carrying these?" one of the other soldiers questioned as he held our toy rifles in his hands.

"We were just playing," Jack said.

"Playing?"

"Playing war. We were hunting down Nazis . . . like our dad," I said.

"Your dad's in the army?"

"He's in the St. Patrick's Regiment . . . he's in Africa," Jack answered.

There was a pause while the one man—the one who was obviously in charge—seemed to be studying us. His face slowly softened.

"Put them down," he said, and we were released.

"Thanks . . . thanks a lot," I stammered as my feet settled back to earth.

"What are your names?"

"I'm Jack and this is George. We're brothers."

"Where do you two live?"

"Just over there," Jack said, pointing in the general direction of the bright lights of the plant.

"We live with our mother," I added.

"And she let the two of you wander around by yourselves at this time of night?"

"She doesn't know we're here. She's working tonight, at the D.I.L. plant, so my brother is watching me."

"Hah! He almost watched the two of you get shot." The soldier laughed. "Running around waving those toys, by all rights you should both be dead."

"Dead?" I gulped.

He held up the two toy guns. "In the dark, at a distance, these look real."

"What are we going to do with them now, sir?" one of the other soldiers asked.

He called him "sir"—that meant he was an officer.

"Should we bring them up to the L.C.?" another suggested.

I didn't know who that was, but I didn't like the sound of being brought anywhere. I just wanted them to let me go home.

"No," the officer said. "They'll get no farther tonight. Maybe we should have somebody drive them back to their home and have a talk with their mother."

"Our mother?" I gulped. "Couldn't we see the L.C. guy instead?"

All of the soldiers started to laugh, and although I didn't really understand why, it was a lot better than being yelled at.

"Put them in the jeep," the officer said.

What did that mean? Where were they taking us? A hand was placed on my arm and Jack and I were walked to the jeep.

"In the back with you," the man said as he boosted me over the side and into the back seat and then climbed in beside me. Jack was put into the front seat.

The officer walked over, leaned in close to the driver and said something that I couldn't hear. The driver then nodded his head and the two of them changed places so that the officer was sitting behind the wheel.

"The two of you stay here and guard the tunnel entrance. We'll be back soon," he said.

He started the engine. It roared and rumbled and the seats shook. The jeep jumped forward, forcing my head back.

"Where are we going?" I asked. "Where are you taking us?"

"You'll see soon enough," the soldier sitting beside me said. "Enjoy the ride while you can."

The jeep's headlights formed a column of light up and along the road. The vehicle picked up speed, and I bounced up and down over the unseen bumps and ruts.

"Hold on," the soldier ordered, and I grabbed onto the seat with both hands just as we hit a particularly big bump and I became airborne.

"I told you to hold on!" he laughed.

I tightened my grip on the seat as we continued to bounce along the track. Just how far were they taking us? As if in answer the jeep's engine groaned and whined as it changed gears and started to slow down. I scanned the surrounding darkness. There didn't seem to be anything there. The jeep came to a full stop.

"Get out," the soldier ordered, and I climbed awkwardly over the side and scrambled over to stand beside Jack. The two soldiers climbed out as well.

"The highway is that way," the officer said, pointing in the direction we'd been travelling.

"We can just leave?" I asked.

"Get going. And I don't want to see either of you back here again, do you understand?"

"Yes . . . yes . . . we understand," I stammered.

"You're lucky you're both not dead. Now go!"

Jack grabbed me by the arm and we started walking away.

"Wait!" the officer called out before we'd taken even a half dozen steps.

Oh God, it was all supposed to be over, and now what? We stopped and turned around to face them once again.

"I need to know your last name," the officer called out.

"Braun," my brother said.

"Did you say Brown?" he asked.

"No . . . Braun."

"Braun. That sounds German," the soldier said.

"Our grandfather was German," Jack told him.

"So just which side is your father fighting for in Africa?" He laughed.

I felt the hairs on the back of my neck stand on end. What was Jack going to say? Surely even Jack wouldn't dare to say anything to a couple of soldiers who were—

"You're lucky my father *is* in Africa," Jack snapped. "Because if he was here he'd beat the *snot* out of you two zombies!"

"We aren't zombies!" the soldier exclaimed.

Zombies were soldiers who had been forced to join the army instead of volunteering, like our father. Usually they kept them at home and away from the action.

"If you're not zombies, then why aren't you fighting against the Nazis?" Jack demanded.

"We're here because—"

"Enough!" yelled the officer. "Don't push your luck, kid! Now both of you get going before I change my mind about the whole thing . . . and I don't ever want to see either of you again!"

I grabbed Jack by the arm. For a split second he resisted, standing there, glaring at the two soldiers. But I pulled harder and he turned and started to come with me. I stumbled forward and practically tripped over a small rut in the road. My legs felt heavy and stiff. I looked back over my shoulder. All I could see were the two headlights of the jeep. The two men were silhouetted in the lights. I turned back around. We kept moving, farther and farther, until the road became dark.

"What were you trying to do back there?" I hissed at my brother.

"Nobody insults our family," he snapped.

"They were soldiers . . . with guns!"

"I don't care if it was Hitler himself!"

Up ahead in the distance a car whizzed by, and then another. That had to be the highway. I had to fight the urge to race away.

"Do you want to run?" I asked.

"Maybe a little," Jack said. "We'd better get home before Mom calls. Those soldiers were a bit scary . . . but not as scary as Mom."

Despite everything I couldn't help but laugh. Jack sprinted away and I ran along beside him, not daring to let him get away. I was just grateful to leave behind whatever it was we were running from. We soon reached the highway, but neither of us slowed down. We turned onto the side of the road and just kept running.

"Jack, are you asleep?" I asked.

"Nope. Thinking."

"About what happened tonight?"

"Of course about what happened tonight."

"And what do you think?" I asked.

"I don't know. I was just trying to figure out who those guys were."

"What do you mean? They were soldiers."

"Don't think so. Those weren't regular army uniforms," he said.

"Could be air force," I suggested.

"But they didn't look like that either."

As I thought about it I knew Jack was right. We had both seen enough pictures of men in the different branches of the service to recognize the uniforms.

"I'm not sure who those guys were," Jack said. "And I'm not sure what's going on up there."

"Maybe we should ask Mom," I offered.

"Don't be stupid!" Jack barked. "Do you know how much trouble we'd be in if she heard about what happened?"

"I guess you're right."

We'd gotten home just as the phone was ringing and Jack had rushed in and answered it. He'd told Mom that we'd been just outside—"fooling around in the backyard"—when she'd called the first time. He hadn't told her anything about what had happened.

"Maybe we should go back and check it out," Jack said.

"Are you crazy?" I demanded. "Whoever those guys were they had guns, real guns, and they told us not to go back."

"Well . . . I was just curious."

"You can stay curious. There's no way I'm heading back down that road or through that particular field again . . . ever."

"I guess you're right," Jack agreed.

"Of course I'm right."

"Now stop bothering me and go to sleep," he muttered.

I did stop bothering him, but I didn't think there was any way I was getting to sleep for a long time.

# CHAPTER THREE

"COME ON BOYS, TIME to get up."

"What time is it, Mom?" I asked as I sat up.

"Almost seven o'clock."

"Seven o'clock!" Jack said. "Why are you getting us up so early?"

"Because I have to get to work soon," she said. She sounded really tired, but she was already dressed in her work clothes, with her dark brown hair pinned up.

"But you're on the afternoon shift. You don't have to be at work until four," I said as I stretched.

"Not today. Edna Smith needed to be off this afternoon—something about going to see one of her sons play baseball—so she asked if we could switch."

"Does that mean you'll be home for supper tonight?" I asked.

She nodded her head.

That was good news. Rather than leaving something for Jack to heat up and serve us, she'd be making supper.

"You two seem awfully sleepy," Mom said. "Were you up late last night?"

"No, we got to bed early, didn't we, George."

"Yeah, early," I said, nodding my head in agreement. Early, like early in the morning after midnight. Then it was hours after that before I'd managed to drift off. I'd been too revved up to get to sleep.

"Then you both should be well rested," Mom said. Something about the tone of her voice left little question that she doubted what we had just told her.

"I do feel well rested," I said as I quickly swung my feet over the side of the mattress. "How about you, Jack?"

"I'm just raring to go," he said, practically jumping out of bed.

Mom really didn't like leaving us alone while she was at work. She had even threatened to get somebody to babysit us. But though I didn't much like having Jack take care of me, I really hated the idea of anybody else doing it. Somebody else might have been responsible. Not like Jack. With Jack in charge, it meant that we could do pretty well anything we wanted. Or I guess, really, whatever Jack wanted. Thank goodness he almost always wanted to do something fun.

"If you get dressed and come to the kitchen right now there might just be a hot breakfast waiting for you," Mom said.

"Hot breakfast?" Jack asked hopefully.

I took a deep breath. "Like in pancakes or biscuits?"

Mom smiled. "You've got a good nose there," she said.

I smiled back. But sniffing out food really wasn't hard. The house was so small that you could smell or hear everything going on everywhere. I was surprised I hadn't heard her up and moving around when she was making breakfast. I guess I really was tired.

She left the room and we started to get dressed. Jack pulled out a clean shirt from his dresser. I reached down between my bed and the wall and grabbed some clothes that I'd already worn. I rummaged around until I found my favourite shirt and started to pull it on.

"You're not going to wear that again, are you?" Jack asked.

"Why not? I'm saving soap and water," I said.

Before the war, wearing the same thing all the time would have made me a slob—now I was being patriotic by saving valuable resources.

"You thinking about last night?" Jack asked.

"Not really. I *was* thinking about hot biscuits."

"I even dreamed about it," he said. "But I still can't figure out what those guys were up to."

"I think it's just some sort of base, and they don't want a couple of kids hanging around there."

"But why wasn't it marked, why weren't there high fences, and why didn't those soldiers wear regular uniforms—if they even were soldiers?"

"Of course they were soldiers. What else would they be?" I asked.

"I don't know," he admitted reluctantly. "But you know what I do know?"

"What? What do you know?"

"If you don't get to the kitchen quick I'm going to eat your share of the biscuits!"

Jack rushed out of the room, and I scrambled to pull on my second sock, half bouncing and jumping on one foot, and hurried after him. By the time I got there he was already sitting at the kitchen table, piling pancakes onto his plate.

"Leave some for me, will you!" I demanded.

"There's plenty for both of you," Mom said. "Do you two have to fight about everything?"

I looked at Jack and he looked at me and we both shrugged.

"Yeah, I think we have to," he said.

I nodded in agreement. "We *are* brothers."

"How do you ever get along together when I'm away at work?" she asked.

"We do fine," I said.

"Great! We do great!" Jack insisted. "You don't have to worry about us."

"Not at all," I added in agreement.

"I still think that maybe I should ask that nice older woman from down the road to look in on the two of you while I'm at—"

"No!" we both practically yelled in unison.

"I'm looking after him," Jack said.

"He's doing a good job. A really good job!"

"And you aren't fighting too much?"

"Not at all," I said. "We're not fighting at all!"

My mother gave me a look like she didn't believe me.

"Maybe a little bit," I said. "But not much, really."

"He's telling the truth," Jack told her. "We get along great, me and my baby brother."

"I'm not a baby, you—" I stopped myself mid sentence. "Could you pass the butter . . . I mean the margarine?" I asked instead.

My mother passed me down the plate holding the margarine. I cut off a small piece—it had a strange orangey colour and didn't look anything like butter—and put it on top of my pancakes.

"That stuff doesn't taste right," Jack said. "I just wish we had syrup and then I wouldn't care about butter."

"I can't get what isn't available," my mother said apologetically.

"We're not blaming you," Jack told her.

"We know rationing makes it hard to get stuff," I added.

Butter and eggs and sugar—which meant syrup—were all in short supply because of the war. Every family was entitled to a certain amount each month of the rationed items, but even then sometimes the stores ran out, and there was nothing that could be done.

I cut up the pancakes and put a piece in my mouth. Good—but not great. Still, I knew that my mother did the best she could with what she could get.

"It was so different when we were at home on the farm," Jack sighed.

"I know . . . I know," Mom agreed.

That's what probably made things even worse for us about some of the rationing. When we'd lived on the farm we'd had all the eggs and butter we could ever have wanted. Coming here had been hard—but there hadn't been any choice, really. With Dad gone off to fight we couldn't very well run the farm. Instead, when an opportunity came up to work at the munitions factory Mom just grabbed it. She leased out our fields to neighbouring farmers. They would work them until the war was over and Dad came back and we could all return to the farm again.

"So what are you two going to be up to today while I'm at work?"

"We found these two old car inner tubes yesterday," Jack said.

"Where did you find those?"

"Just around . . . in the field," Jack lied.

"You just found a couple of inner tubes?" Mom asked suspiciously. Rubber was another one of the things that was in short supply because of the war.

"They were really, really old and in bad shape," Jack explained.

We'd actually found them in a pile of old tires stacked up at the back of a junkyard on the other side of town—another place we probably shouldn't have gone.

"And what are you going to do with two tubes that are *really, really old and in bad shape?*" Mum asked.

"We patched them up so they'll hold air."

"At least we think we think they'll hold air," I said.

"We're going to go up to the gas station and use the air hose to pump them up and then go down to Corbett's Creek for a swim."

"Just the two of you?"

Jack shrugged. "There might be some other kids there."

"You could invite some other kids to go along," she suggested.

I knew where this was going.

"There's nothing wrong with you two making some new friends," she went on.

"We didn't say there was," Jack answered.

"There are lots of kids all around who are the same age as the two of you," she added. "You should talk to them."

"We've talked to kids," Jack said. We'd tried—they weren't that friendly. Leaving the farm had also meant leaving our friends behind. Though I guess it was more like leaving Jack's friends behind. I'd had friends at school, but mostly I'd just hung around with Jack and his buddies.

"We've even played with kids on the street," I said. Not much, but we had.

"I'd better get going," Mom said. "The bus to the plant leaves in twenty minutes. Are you going to do your papers before or after you go swimming?"

"Before."

"It doesn't take too long because I help him," I said.

"Less than an hour," Jack said. "Especially if we rush."

She came over and gave first Jack and then me a little kiss on the top of the head. "Be good, and take care of each other."

"Bye, Mom!"

"See you tonight!" Jack called out.

The door had hardly closed when Jack got up from the table and went into the cupboard. He pulled out a bag of semi-dried banana strips, reached in and took out a piece, stuffing it in his mouth.

"Do you want some?" he asked, offering me the package.

I shook my head. "I really don't like the taste of those any more than I like the taste of the margarine."

While eggs and sugar were in short supply, things like bananas were impossible to get. Anything that had to come from the tropics, like rubber or bananas, just wasn't available any more. Instead we had these dried banana strips.

"At least they're sweet," Jack said as he crunched on another piece. "So the plan for the day is to clean up, do the papers and head down for a swim."

I snuggled down into the inner tube. My arms and legs dangled in the cool water. It felt so good. I closed my eyes and just let the world float by.

"Doesn't this remind you of home?" Jack asked.

"It does," I agreed, opening my eyes and looking first at him and then around us. It was calm and quiet—like where we lived . . . where we used to live. There was a creek running right through our farm, and when we'd finished all our chores Jack and I would go for a swim. I really missed it.

Of course we weren't alone in being new here in Whitby. Almost everybody on the whole street was new. People had moved from all over the country to work at the munitions factory, making bullets, and tons of new homes had been built for all of us to live in. They were all prefabricated houses constructed by the Wartime Housing Corporation. All exactly the same—two bedrooms, no basement, one storey, on a little piece of land. They all looked so similar that for the first week we lived here I couldn't figure out which house was even ours. Once I even walked up to the wrong house and walked in the front door. Thank goodness nobody was home and I saw the furniture, realized it wasn't our house and left before anybody noticed.

It was all so different from our farmhouse. Our house was really old and made of stones from the fields and timbers from our forest. And it was so big that you could be in one part of the house without hearing everything that was going on everywhere else . . . not like here.

"I could just stay here all day," Jack said, spinning a bit in his tube under the hot sun.

"We could do that. Mom isn't going to be home for hours and hours and hours."

Jack just smiled. "Let's get out of the current or we'll drift all the way down to the lake. Follow me."

We both started using our arms to paddle. Jack aimed toward a little island in the middle of the creek. He and his inner tube partially disappeared underneath the branches of a large weeping willow that dominated the little chunk of land. Its branches reached right down to the surface of the water. I floated in after him, and I was immediately struck by how much cooler it felt in the shade of the tree.

"This is perfect," Jack said. He was hanging on to some of the branches.

I reached up and grabbed a branch, looping it around my wrist. The current wasn't very strong and I was held in place. I closed my eyes and enjoyed the quiet of the day. It was hard to find quiet where we lived now. There was always something close by—a person or a car or even an airplane flying overhead.

"How far are we from Lake Ontario?" I asked.

"Not too far I don't think. You see the bridge there?"

I looked over my shoulder and between the branches dangling down into the water. I could make out a wooden bridge in the distance, crossing over the creek.

"That's the railroad bridge," Jack told me. "Those are the tracks we were climbing up to last night."

A shiver ran up my spine. Lying there, massaged by the gentle water, I'd momentarily forgotten about yesterday. And that was strange because I'd spent a good part of the day thinking about it.

"Do you see that?" Jack asked.

"See what?"

"There's somebody on the bridge."

I spun around so I was facing the bridge. There was somebody—it looked like a man—standing at the very centre.

"What do you think he's doing?" I asked.

"Probably just doing what we were trying to do yesterday, taking a shortcut," Jack suggested.

"But he's just standing there looking over the edge and—there's another man!"

A second person had appeared on the bridge—they looked the same, dressed all in black. And then a third man joined them.

"They must be some sort of railroad crew," Jack said.

"That makes sense," I agreed. "They must be inspecting the tracks."

Suddenly a fourth man appeared, dressed in the same manner. But instead of being on the top like the others he was climbing on the trestles. As he started to climb up, two of the men on the bridge climbed down to meet him.

"What are they doing now?" I asked.

He shook his head. "I can't really tell . . . are they putting something on the bridge?"

"I can't really see . . . it looks like some sort of . . . I don't know, almost like pieces of wood or something." There were dark patches on the wood now where something had been put in place.

"No, not wood . . ." Jack said.

"Whatever it is, they must be guys who do bridge repairs."

"I guess," he agreed, though he didn't sound too sure.

"What else could it be?"

Jack didn't say anything, but he had a look on his face, the one that always made me think he knew things I didn't.

"Maybe," I suggested, "if we got closer we could—"

"No," he snapped, cutting me off. "I want to stay right here where they can't see us."

"Why don't you want them to see us?"

"I don't know," he said, shaking his head. "I just want to stay out of sight."

Jack's being nervous made me feel nervous.

"Are you sure we can't be seen here?" I asked.

"As long as we stay here we're invisible."

That was reassuring.

"Look what they're doing now," Jack said.

I tried to look around the branches. The four men were moving back and forth across the supports of the bridge.

"They're putting up wires, I think," he said. "You see what that one at the top is holding?"

I stared at him hard. It was a large, round object . . . sort of like a gigantic spool of thread.

"That's a spool that holds wire. They're definitely attaching wire to the bridge."

"Could wire help hold up a bridge?" I asked.

"They're not putting that wire there to hold up the bridge."

"What do you mean?"

"Those men aren't here to repair the bridge . . . I think they're here to blow it up."

# CHAPTER FOUR

"QUIT JOKING AROUND, JACK," I said nervously.

"I'm not joking." His tone was quiet and serious.

"Why would anybody blow up a bridge?"

"Not *anybody*. Enemy agents. Don't you remember that newsreel we saw last month about saboteurs?"

We'd gone to the movies, and before the feature film they'd shown a newsreel about the war and then a cartoon about watching for "enemy activity" here at home.

"Jack, this isn't a movie, this is real life," I pointed out.

"Look what they're doing," Jack said.

The four men were leaving the bridge. The last one was walking backwards, holding onto that spool—it looked almost like a big reel from a fishing rod.

"He's laying the wire to lead to the detonator."

"Come on, Jack, you can't know that," I said.

"I know things. I'm fourteen years old. I've seen stuff. I've read stuff."

As we watched, the last man scrambled over the near side of the embankment, leaving the tracks behind. He slipped and slid down, rocks sliding under his feet. Then he joined the other three men, taking shelter behind a large boulder.

"That's why they're hiding behind the rock, because they're going to blow it up," Jack said.

"Why would anybody want to blow up *this* bridge?"

"Think, George!" he hissed. "This is the main railroad line to Toronto. And it goes right through the yard of the munitions factory."

"The factory where Mom works?"

He nodded his head.

"If you're right, shouldn't we do something?" I pleaded.

"Like what?"

"I don't know, maybe go for help."

"Can you still see those men?" Jack asked.

"Of course I can."

"Then if you tried to leave they'd see you. We're only safe as long as we stay right here under the tree."

"Even if they did see us we could still get away. We'd just outrun them."

"You can't outrun a bullet," he said grimly.

"They have guns?" Suddenly I felt very afraid. "I didn't see any guns."

"Neither did I, but if they're Nazi agents, don't you think they'd have guns? We have to stay here."

"For how long?"

"I don't know . . . until they're gone."

"Yeah, and the bridge is blown up. What if we went that way and then through the woods?" I asked.

"That wouldn't work. As soon as we hit open water they'd see us . . . we'd be dead before we hit the trees."

"Come on, Jack, please stop saying things like that."

"I'm not saying anything that isn't true. We have to stay here. Maybe they'll go away before the bridge blows . . . maybe they're going to use a timer."

"What's a timer?" I asked.

"It's a thing like a clock. They set it so the bomb explodes later."

"And they've got one of those?"

"How would I know?" Jack said, angrily. "I just know that there *are* things like that."

"So if they're gone we can go and get help. Maybe we can find somebody who can disconnect the bomb, like the police, or they can call for the military to come."

"Or maybe *we* could disconnect it," Jack said.

"What?" I couldn't believe he was even thinking that.

"We could disconnect it. I think we just have to pull out the wires."

"You're crazy! We can't do that!"

"But what if a train comes before we can get help and—" He stopped and cocked his head to the side.

"What? What's wrong?"

"Listen," he said.

Immediately I heard what he was hearing. It was a low, rumbling sound that could mean only one thing.

"There's a train coming." Jack's voice was barely a whisper.

"Can you tell which direction it's coming from?"

He shook his head.

"Do you think it could be from the factory?" I asked.

"I told you I don't know! I can't see it. I can only hear it. It's coming."

The sound was growing louder, and I could feel the vibrations through the tree. Even the water was starting to tremble.

"Come here," Jack said.

"What?"

"Come here and get out of the tube," he said as he slipped over the side of his and into the waist-deep water.

"But—"

"Don't argue with me, just get into the water!" he ordered.

I slid into the water and waded over beside him, towing the inner tube with me and looking over my shoulder as I moved. The train still wasn't in sight, but the sound was nearly deafening now.

"Why did we get into the water?" I had to shout to be heard.

"It'll protect us."

"Protect us from what?"

"The explosion, idiot."

"We're far away. It can't be that big . . . they couldn't have put that much explosive stuff on the bridge."

"Ammunition," I heard him say. And he was right. What if the train was carrying ammunition? What would it be like if a train filled with ammunition exploded? I tried to picture it. It would be tremendous . . . unbelievable . . . it would fill the sky and . . .

"We have to get farther away," I blurted out.

"There isn't time," Jack said, and he pointed.

I looked up. It was a freight train, and it was coming from the direction of the plant!

"Just do what I do!" Jack yelled over the noise.

I followed him to shore and tossed my tube onto a little lip of land right beside where he tossed his. Although it felt stupid I reached out and took his hand.

The train came close, the big engine growling and rumbling, the noise echoing down the creek, closed in by the trees and banks. It reached the edge of the bridge and I held my breath and . . . it kept coming, the second car, and then the next and the next. With each car there was a loud *thump, thump* as the axles hit the bridge. When were they going to set off the explosion? Were they waiting for the very middle of the train? Maybe that was where they kept the ammunition cars. I looked at Jack wide-eyed.

"I don't know!" he screamed over the noise.

I turned back to look. Car after car it came, each one thumping across the bridge. The caboose was already in sight. Maybe they were trying to kill the crew! It came closer and closer and then hit the bridge, and in a second it was gone. It was over the bridge, moving farther down the track, getting smaller and smaller, taking the noise with it until it was just a soft hum and then a slight vibration in the water and then . . . nothing.

"What happened?" I whispered to Jack.

"Maybe they didn't hook it up right." He paused. "Look, they're going back."

The four men had started to climb back up the embankment and onto the tracks. As they walked, two of them were rolling up the wire that they'd laid out. Why were they doing that? If it hadn't been hooked up right, wouldn't they just check things and get the next train?

From our hiding spot we could see the men, and now we could hear them, too. Before they had been completely silent, but now they were laughing and talking in loud voices. The train had gotten by, so why were they so happy? It seemed like the more we watched the less sense everything made.

As two of the men stood in the middle of the bridge, two started down the sides, climbing along the trestle beams. These two were unwinding the wires, threading them back through the beams while the two at the top pulled them back up. Jack and I watched wordlessly for close to five minutes until finally all the wires were removed, and all four men reassembled on the top.

"They haven't removed the explosives yet," Jack said.

I could clearly see that the dark blobs still remained attached to the support beams of the bridge.

"Maybe they take the wires first and then go back for them," I said.

"Maybe, but I'm not so—oh my goodness," Jack hissed.

At that same instant I saw what he saw—a black inner tube was floating down the creek toward the bridge. I turned around; only one of ours was still pushed partially up on the shore.

"You idiot, you should have put your tube higher up."

"*My* tube? How do you know it's not yours!" I protested.

"Sssssshhhhh . . . keep it down. It doesn't matter whose it is. I just hope they don't see it."

"What could happen if they do?"

He shook his head. "I don't know, but maybe they might come looking for where it came from."

A shiver, unrelated to the cold of the creek, ran through my entire body.

While I watched the men perched atop the bridge, I kept one eye on the inner tube. It was bobbing down the creek . . . slowly twirling and bouncing along with the current. It was almost like it was dancing, getting closer and closer to the bridge, and still they hadn't seen it. In just a few seconds it would be right underneath their feet and then it would pop out the other side and—it hit one of the supports! The tube spun around to the side, pushed by the current, and then stopped moving. It seemed to be stuck, wedged in against the wooden beam.

I looked up at the men and was shocked to see that they were no longer there. I quickly turned my head and spotted them walking along the tracks, away from the bridge. Then they dropped off the far side of the embankment, disappearing from my view.

"They didn't take the explosives," Jack said, excited. "They left them attached."

"We'd better go and get help," I said. "We'd better tell somebody."

"We'd better get your inner tube."

"How do you know it's even *my* . . . no, forget it, we have to go and get help!"

"We'll go *after* we get the tube."

"Let's just leave it!" I pleaded. "It isn't that important."

"Maybe not to you."

He waded over, grabbed the second tube, threw it in the water and flung himself on to it.

There were just a few seconds to decide as he floated by. I grabbed onto the side of the tube. The branches of the willow tree brushed against us as we drifted through them and into the open water of the creek.

I was instantly hit by two things: the hot, bright rays of the sun and the realization that we were now completely exposed to anybody watching the river. I ducked down further into the water to escape both the heat and any eyes that might be trained on the water.

"Are you sure they're gone?"

"They're gone . . . for now," Jack said.

This was crazy. Why were we risking being seen to get some patched-up, old inner tube? Then I realized that it wasn't the tube Jack wanted. It was just an excuse to get a closer look.

There was a slight dip in the creek and we picked up speed as we neared the bridge. I looked up but couldn't see the very top any more. I let go of the tube at almost the same second as Jack jumped off. He towed the tube behind him as we both swam for the side, the place where the other tube was trapped. The current lessened and the water became shallow. My feet touched bottom and I waded over to the side. I grabbed the inner tube and flipped it over. It had a small red mark by the valve. It *was* my inner tube.

"Hold onto this," Jack said, pushing his tube toward me.

I grabbed it. Why did he want me to hold his tube? In answer to my unasked question he put one foot on the bottom support of the bridge and heaved himself up and out of the water.

"What are you doing?" I demanded.

"I need to see something up close."

"See what?"

He didn't answer, but I already knew what he wanted to see. He started up the trestle, climbing from support to support. I wanted to call out, but I didn't. This was crazy! What if he fell, or those men came back or . . . something exploded? Even if the wires weren't attached, they were still explosives!

"Please come down, Jack!" I hissed as loud as I dared.

He was perched beside one of the dark patches. It looked like a big lump of clay. He reached out a hand toward it!

"Jack, don't!"

I looked up at him. He'd taken some of it and he seemed to be studying it and—

"Uuugggg!" I screamed in shock as something fell down and hit me in the face.

"It's just clay!" Jack called down. "Clay! Here, catch!"

He dropped another chunk, and without even thinking I reached out and grabbed it. I played around with it. Clay. It was clay.

"They're all clay!"

I looked up at Jack. He'd moved along the supports and was holding more clay in his hand. He let it go, and it dropped into the water with a large splash.

He climbed down the supports, finally slipping into the water and swimming over to my side.

"Do you understand what happened?" I asked.

He shook his head. "Nope . . . but I'm tired of not knowing, so I'm going to find out."

# CHAPTER FIVE

"JACK, WE SHOULD BE going home."

"We will go home. After I've got some answers."

"I just don't think we should be doing this!"

"Make sure you stash your inner tube high enough up on the shore so it doesn't wash away this time."

He always knew what to say to shut me up. I was sure I wouldn't be hearing the end of that for a long time. I pushed the tube further up the bank, away from the edge of the creek.

"It would be better if we had our shoes, at least," I said, trying to throw up some excuses. "Couldn't we come tomorrow and bring shoes?"

"Good idea. Today we won't have shoes and tomorrow, when we come back, we'll have shoes."

"I meant we could just come tomorrow!" I explained.

"Do you really think we'll be able to find out everything in this one trip?"

"No, I guess there'll be some things that . . . wait, what makes you think I'm coming back here again?"

"Because if I'm coming, then you're coming," Jack said. "Unless you want that old lady from up the street to watch you."

I had to hand it to him. He got me again.

I trailed behind my brother as he picked his way along a path leading away from the creek. It was a small, beaten-down trail, mainly mud with an occasional rock embedded in it that managed to find the tender spots in the arches of my feet. The path came to a stop in front of a wire fence. It was about four feet high, with one strand of barbed wire at the top. On the other side was a field. There were lots of bushes sprouting up everywhere, and the grass was waist high. It hadn't been grazed or worked for a long time.

"Should we go along the fence?" I asked, though I knew what was coming next.

Jack put his foot on one strand of wire, pushing it down while he grabbed the piece right above it, pulling it up. Reluctantly I ducked down and climbed through the hole. I straightened up and tried to do the same for him. The wire was taut and dug into my bare foot.

"Push harder," Jack said as he wriggled through.

"Do you really think we should do this?" I asked.

"I don't think the cows are going to mind," Jack said.

"There hasn't been anything in here for a long time," I said, looking around.

"That's why I don't think they're going to mind."

"That isn't what I meant. Anyway, I don't think we should be following those men."

"We're not following them . . . we're just slowly headed in the same direction, that's all."

I knew that arguing with him wasn't going to work. Arguing with Jack never worked. I shut my mouth. It was better that we moved without making a noise. Better because nothing could hear us, and I could hear other things more clearly.

Jack led us straight across the field to a wooded patch. The instant we got into the shade, I felt better. The cover of the trees protected us from more than just the sun.

"Do you know where we're going?" I asked.

He motioned with his head. "We're following that."

Off to our left, just barely visible through the trees, was the railroad embankment. We were moving along parallel to it. That was reassuring. As long as we stayed on this route we'd be able to find our way back to the creek when he came to his senses and said we could start home.

Past the woods was another field, this one much bigger. It had to be close to fifty yards wide, and the grass was beaten down. Whatever was using this field was using it well.

"That is really something," Jack said.

I looked around anxiously. I didn't see anything. What was he talking about?

"Must be a couple of hundred feet high." He was pointing up and into the distance.

I looked up. Towering above the horizon was an antenna, stretching up into the sky.

"Wow, it's gigantic. What is it for?" I asked.

"Radio. What else?"

"It looks really high. It could get messages from all over."

"And send them."

"What do you mean?" I asked.

"The same aerial that receives radio signals can send them as well. But maybe it isn't as high as it looks. The only way to tell is to get closer."

"I don't think that's smart," I said.

"Not smart? I guess you'd be an expert at not being smart. Come on, let's go," and he started to walk out from the cover of the trees.

"We can't just walk across that field."

"You're right."

"Good, let's head back and—"

"We'll go around it," Jack said, cutting me off. "Do you want to go to the left or the right?"

I didn't want to go either way, but at least to the left was the familiar outline of the embankment. "Let's go left."

Jack took the lead again. The trees gave way to bushes and shrubs. We picked our way through at the very edge of the field. As long as there was cover I was happy.

"There's a little creek," Jack said. "Let's get a drink."

It was more like a trickle then a creek, water running along a little rocky bed. I crouched down and took a seat on one of the bigger rocks. I cupped my hands and brought up a mouthful of water. It was cold and felt good going down. Jack sat down on a rock beside me and did the same.

"How far are we going to go?" I asked.

"I was going to turn around a while ago."

"What?" I groaned. "Why didn't you?"

"You started bugging me so I figured I wouldn't," Jack explained. "And then I saw that big antenna and wanted to check it out."

"Do you think that . . . " I stopped as I realized that there was no point in saying anything. "Do you think that we could have more water before we go on?" I asked instead.

Jack smiled. "Have as much as you want."

I bent down and slurped up another handful. I moved my bottom around on the rock so that my feet were in the small flow of water as well.

"Do you hear anything?" Jack asked.

I pricked up my ears. I could hear something. "Is it another train?"

Jack shook his head. "Not a train . . . wrong direction and wrong sound. I think it's a car."

"Or a jeep?"

Jack didn't say a word, but his face gave away the answer to my question. He slithered off the rock we were sitting on and I did the same, using it for cover.

"Can you see anything?" I whispered, peering around the rock and through the bushes and trees that stood between the field and us.

"Nothing . . . but it's coming closer."

There was no mistaking that. The rumbling sound was getting louder and louder. Even without seeing it, I could picture it in my mind: a jeep carrying two soldiers, one carrying a rifle, the second with his weapon at his side. What would they say to us if they caught us again? More important, what would they do to us?

I looked around the rock and caught a glimpse of the vehicle—it *was* a jeep—as it flashed by. The sound started to fade and there was a squealing noise . . . brakes! It was stopping! The pitch of the engine changed, then it started to get louder once more, and then it stopped completely. They'd stopped!

I looked over at Jack. He was pressed down tightly to the ground and his head was turned away from me. I reached out and tapped him on the shoulder. He turned and mouthed the words "Don't move." He was right . . . we had to stay still. There was no way they could have seen us yet . . . was there?

"Identify yourself!" yelled a man, and I almost jumped into the air in response.

"Come out with your hands up!" called out a second male voice.

I looked over at Jack. His eyes were pressed tightly closed.

"If you don't come out *now* we're going to shoot!"

"Jack . . . we have to!" I hissed at him.

He opened his eyes and nodded. There was no choice. I was just going to stand up when off to the side four men dressed in black stood up first, their hands in the air! I looked at Jack and he looked at me and we dropped back down to the ground.

"Come out slowly with your hands in plain view!" one of the men shouted.

Jack had wriggled around and was sitting up behind a bush. Quickly I crawled over and joined him. Through the bush and the scrub up ahead we could see the scene being played out. The four men, obviously the men from the bridge, were slowly coming forward toward two soldiers standing at the edge of the field in front of a jeep with their rifles levelled right at them. I recognized one of the soldiers from the night before!

"They caught them," I whispered. "They caught them!"

"They're not carrying anything," Jack hissed.

"What do you mean?"

"The spool of wire . . . they've ditched it somewhere, and—"

*"Sprechen Sie Deutsch?"* called out one of the soldiers loudly.

"What does that mean?" I whispered to Jack.

"I don't know . . . *Deutsch* . . . isn't that German?"

I strained my mind trying to think of the few words in German that our Opa, our father's father, had taught us.

*"Ja, wir sprechen deutsch,"* called back one of the four men in black.

There was that word again. "They're Germans!" I hissed at Jack. "They really are German agents!"

One of the soldiers barked out a command. I didn't understand what he was saying, so it must have been in German, but the four men all responded, lowering their hands and placing them on the tops of their heads instead. There was another order given and the four men dropped to their knees, their hands still locked together.

One of the soldiers lowered his rifle while the second man stepped back, his weapon still aimed at the men. The first soldier launched into a series of rapid questions.

"He's interrogating them," Jack said.

"What's to know?" I asked. "They're German secret agents who just tried to destroy a railroad bridge."

"With mud for bombs," Jack said.

"Oh, yeah, that's right."

"Besides, they probably don't know anything about what happened on the bridge or they would have stopped them there."

Of course he was right about that too. "Maybe we should tell them."

"Don't be stupid," Jack hissed. "We're not supposed to be here *either*. Just watch and stop talking."

The soldier walked back and forth in front of the four men. He barked out questions I couldn't understand and they answered back. He stopped in front of one of the men and bent over and started yelling at him. The man shook his head repeatedly but wasn't answering. The soldier drew back his hand and slapped him, sending him reeling backwards!

I gasped in shock.

Jack looked over at me. "Serves him right," he whispered. "That's the way you have to treat Nazis and enemy agents."

The man picked himself up and returned to the same position as the others, on his knees.

The soldier barked out another order and slowly the four men, hands still on top of their heads, rose to their feet.

Another order was given and the four men turned around, facing away from the soldiers. The soldier who had been doing all the speaking retrieved his rifle, and now both soldiers trained their weapons on the men.

"What are they doing?" I asked.

"I . . .think . . . they're going to shoot them," Jack stammered. "They can't do that . . . they can't . . . can they?"

One of the soldiers lowered his rifle and then the second did the same. They started to laugh, and then the four men lowered their hands and turned around. They started to laugh as well! They walked toward the soldiers. One of them reached out and hugged one of them! It was the man who'd been slapped! They laughed and talked and smiled and slapped each other on the back and . . . this was unbelievable . . . what was happening?

I turned to Jack. He looked totally stunned.

One of the soldiers handed his rifle to one of the men dressed in black. He walked over and climbed behind the wheel of the jeep. The second soldier climbed into the seat beside him. The four men, one still holding on to the rifle, piled into the back, two filling the seats, the other two standing, holding onto the big roll bar. The engine roared to life and the gears ground together as the jeep started off. We stayed hidden behind the bush, not moving, as the jeep bumped across the field, getting smaller and smaller until it disappeared behind a stand of trees and was gone.

"Jack . . . I . . . don't understand," I stammered. My mind

was filled with raw emotions and thoughts, none of which made any sense. "What just happened?"

Jack just shrugged and shook his head. "I don't know. But I know we have to get out of here."

# CHAPTER SIX

"LOOK, WE CAN TALK about it all you want and it still won't make any sense!" Jack said.

"I just think there has to be some explanation as to why they were speaking German."

"Okay, explain it to me."

"Well, let's just assume that you were right and those four men were spies, and . . . and . . . "

"And what?" Jack demanded.

"Well . . . I guess that I can't really figure it out right now, but maybe—"

"Maybe nothing! All I know is that I want you to shut up about it!" Jack hollered.

"Boys! Boys! No fighting!"

I turned around. It was Mr. Krum, the owner and editor of the local newspaper, the *Whitby Reporter*. Jack and I were sitting on the loading dock at the back of the newspaper office, folding up the papers he'd be delivering today.

"We're not fighting," Jack said. "We're sort of discussing things."

"If this is a discussion, I'd hate to see a fight. It is not polite to say *shut up* to someone."

"Someone? No, you don't understand. I was saying it to my *brother,*" Jack explained with a grin.

Mr. Krum burst into laughter. "Brothers," he said, shaking his head. "Some things don't change from one generation to the next. And what was it that you were arguing about?"

"About the war," Jack told him.

"There's little room for argument there," he said. "One side is good, the other evil. Perhaps in the history of war there has never been such a clear distinction between the two sides."

"We know that. We were arguing about spies and agents and stuff," I explained. "Do you think there are spies?"

Jack shot me a dirty look.

"In every war there are spies," he answered.

"But around here?" Jack asked.

Mr. Krum shrugged. "Why not around here? The munitions factory is one of the biggest in the country. A perfect target for sabotage. And then down the road no more than twenty miles is Camp Thirty."

"What's that?" I asked.

"A prisoner-of-war camp in Bowmanville. It has over two hundred German prisoners. Some very, very important high-ranking officers are imprisoned there."

"I didn't know about that." I said. "Did you?" I asked Jack.

He shook his head.

"Many people don't. Being the editor of the paper I learn many things. That is my job . . . no?"

"I guess so," Jack agreed.

I loved newspapers. I didn't just read them, I dreamed about what it would be like to be a reporter.

"But I've never heard anything about it," I said, "and I read the paper every day."

"That's wonderful to hear, but this is not the kind of information you will find in a newspaper."

"Why?" I asked.

"Classified. There are certain things I cannot write about because of the war. Things we wouldn't want the enemy to know of."

"You think the enemy reads your paper?" Jack asked him.

"Possibly. And possibly you are the one delivering it to their door each day," Mr. Krum said.

"Me? One of my customers?"

Mr. Krum laughed. It was a friendly laugh. When some people laughed it felt as though they were laughing at you, but not him. "Don't look so surprised."

"But my customers are just regular people, they're not spies!"

"Do you think they'd have a sign up on their door, announcing 'German Spies Live Here'? They'd be a little more clever than that. Any of them could be a German agent. As far as you know, *I* could be a German agent."

"You?" Jack asked.

"Why not? Newspaper editor would be the perfect occupation for a spy. Who else has such liberty to wander around and ask questions and poke his nose in where it doesn't belong? Who knows more about a community than the editor of the local paper?"

"I guess you're right," Jack admitted.

"You probably know all about everybody around here . . . more than anybody else," I ventured.

"I think that *know* should be a past-tense verb."

I shook my head. "I . . . I don't understand."

"*Knew* everybody. I knew everybody, but not now. So many new people, so many changes. There are five times as many people subscribing to my paper now as there were last year," Mr. Krum explained. "So many new people whom I know nothing about."

"People like us," Jack said.

"Exactly. Take your mother, for example. She moved down here with her children. She takes up a job at the very factory that makes munitions. Where better for a spy or a saboteur to take a position?"

"Our mother isn't a spy!" I protested.

"I am not saying that she is . . . although if she were, you two would know nothing about it. All I'm saying is that she could be, and I might never find out, because I know nothing about her or the hundreds of other newcomers in the area."

"Do you know what's going on down by the lake over by Thornton Road?" Jack asked.

"Ah . . . it did not take you boys long to find out about the biggest mystery around these parts."

"There's a mystery?"

"Many, I'm afraid. You're talking about Glenrath."

"Glenrath?"

"That was what the property was called. Two hundred and seventy-five acres extending up from the lake to the railroad tracks in the north, and from Corbett's Creek on one side to Thornton Road on the other."

"Who owns it?" Jack asked.

"It used to be owned by the Sinclair family. But it was sold eight months ago."

"Who bought it?"

"That's an interesting question. Some think it was a branch of the government. Judging by those posted signs restricting entry it probably belongs to the Department of National Defence."

"Probably? You don't know?" I asked.

"*Think* and *know* are two very different things. I know that is what the signs say, and I know there are armed guards who patrol the property."

"Have you ever run into the guards?" I asked.

"I was driving along the highway one day when I saw a gigantic truck filled with lumber turn onto Thornton. Naturally I was curious and followed. At least I followed partway down the road until my way was blocked."

"By a jeep, right?" I blurted out.

"Yes, by two armed men in a jeep and . . ." He stopped. "And how would you know that they would be riding in jeeps?"

"Well . . ." I didn't know what to say.

"We've seen them from the fence," Jack said, coming to my rescue.

Obviously he was as wary as I was of telling Mr. Krum about being confronted by the guards. We'd agreed not to talk to anybody, in case they spoke to our mother.

"I see, you were standing at the fence," he said, although his tone suggested that he didn't believe what Jack had told him.

"So these soldiers jumped from their jeep and ordered me to drive back up the road," Mr. Krum continued. "I questioned them, asking them what authority they had to order me about. One of them held up his rifle and promptly told me he was holding his authority in his hands and I should get out before I regretted not leaving."

"And what did you do?" I asked.

Mr. Krum shrugged. "I left." He paused. "For a while."

"Sounds like you've been back," Jack prompted.

"I've asked questions of different people, and I too have stood by the fence and watched. Most peculiar things are going on."

"Like what?"

"Explosions."

"I haven't heard anything like that," Jack said doubtfully.

"It hasn't been as bad lately. There was one explosion, before your family moved here, which was so forceful it broke the windows on houses throughout the area. Dozens and dozens of houses had broken or cracked windows."

"That must have been an interesting story to write," I said.

"Interesting to write. Unfortunately, nobody would ever read it."

"Why not?"

"As I've mentioned, censorship. I was forbidden to run that story."

"I just don't understand why you can't write what you want," Jack said. "It's your paper."

"Not in times of war. The explosion was big news around here, but before my story got to press I received a telephone call from a man stating that he was with the RCMP. He informed me that the story was classified and that he wasn't on the phone to be interviewed. I was informed that the damage to local houses was caused by a low-flying airplane. He stated, rather impolitely I might add, that I could run the story with that explanation or not run the story at all. I chose not to run the story."

"So," said Jack, "if the RCMP told you not to run the story, then whatever's going on at that place must be connected to the government, right?"

"So you'd assume . . . but a good reporter never assumes."

"How did you even know for sure that the man on the phone was from the RCMP?" I asked.

"Ahhhh . . . good question. You'd make a good reporter."

I beamed.

"The man recited a code, a series of numbers, which identified him as being official."

"But how do *you* know about that code?" I asked.

"Official documents were sent to me and, I assume, every

other editor in the country, to identify official communication censoring a story."

"So lots of people know the code," said Jack. "And anybody who knows the code could have called you."

"I imagine that you are correct."

"But you didn't run the story," I said, "so you must have believed him."

"It sounds as though I made an assumption. Perhaps the next time I am asked to alter or suppress a story I should ask for further corroboration."

"Has that happened often, them asking you not to run a story?" I asked.

"Not too often, but I know how I could guarantee a call."

"How?" Jack wanted to know.

"I could start to ask more questions about the gigantic antenna that's been constructed at the south end of the property."

"That *is* huge!" I agreed.

Mr. Krum furrowed his brow. "You've seen the tower?"

"A bit . . . from a distance."

"That's interesting. It is not visible from any place except the lake. Were you on the lake?"

I didn't know what to say.

"Or perhaps, did you do a little bit more than just stand at the fence?" he asked knowingly.

"A little bit more," Jack admitted.

"I understand your curiosity. A good newspaperman is part Nosy Parker and part town gossip," Mr. Krum said. "I'd love to know what was going on. But you boys must promise not to go back there. The things I know for sure are that those men were carrying rifles and people get shot with rifles, and I cannot afford to have Jack getting shot." He paused. "I would be short a paper delivery boy, and it is hard enough to get reliable workers as it is."

"We'll stay away," Jack told him.

I looked over at him, a bit suspiciously.

"I do not know if I believe you, Jack," Mr. Krum said, voicing my doubt. "But that is certainly the correct answer."

"Would you tell us more if you found anything out?" I asked.

"Certainly. If you two promise to stay away from that property, I promise to share any new information I receive. It is my destiny to be here for the duration of this war, although that was not my wish."

"What do you mean?" I asked.

"I tried to enlist."

"You tried to join the army?"

"I went down to the recruitment office in Toronto and offered my services. They declined."

"But why?" I asked.

"They said I was too old."

He was a tall man with dark hair just beginning to turn silver and muscular arms—probably from hefting heavy bundles of newspapers. "You don't look that old," I said.

"Thank you." He smiled. "I just turned fifty, but a young fifty. Besides, I thought my experience as a soldier would outweigh any difficulties caused by my age."

"You were a soldier before?" Jack asked.

"I fought in the First World War."

"Wow . . . that was so long ago . . . I mean, that's really interesting," I stammered, afraid I'd offended him.

Mr. Krum laughed. "It was a long time ago, but war hasn't changed that much. Besides, I was not hoping to be sent to the front. I thought they could use me in communication . . . something related to being in the newspaper business."

"That would make sense," Jack agreed.

"Do you know what we used to call that war?" Mr. Krum asked.

I shook my head.

"It had two names. 'The Great War' and 'The War to End All Wars.' Both names have proven incorrect."

"How long were you in the army?" I asked.

"Just under four years. I was wounded . . . twice. The second wound to my leg ended my career as a soldier, although it did add to my collection of medals."

"You received medals?" Jack asked.

"Many," Mr. Krum said, nodding his head slowly. "Would you like to see them?"

"You have them here?" I asked.

"In my office. They are not things you throw away. Come."

We put aside the newspapers and followed him back through the loading dock and into the main office. There were other people sorting papers and answering phones and clicking away on typewriters. He opened the door to his office and motioned for us to follow.

"I do not usually show these," he said. "But since we were discussing these things . . ."

He removed a large wooden box from a shelf filled with books, and with his shirt sleeve he brushed off a thick layer of dust. Obviously it had been a long time since anybody had seen them. He opened up the box and my eyes widened at the sight. There had to be a dozen medals, shiny, attached to pieces of faded, but still colourful, ribbon.

"You were a hero," I gasped under my breath.

"Two were for given to me for being unfortunate enough to be wounded. Some for simply being in a battle. But this one," he said, pointing out a large one in the very centre of the medals, shiny and silver with raised edges, "this one is for bravery. Would you like to hold it?"

"Could I?"

He nodded his head. Carefully, almost delicately, he reached down and removed it from the wooden box. He placed it in my hands.

"It's heavier than I thought it would be," I said.

"Turn it over and you can see where it has been inscribed."

Gently I turned it over. There clearly visible, was writing . . . but I couldn't understand the words except for a name: Rainer Krum.

"Who is Rainer?" I asked.

"That is my full name."

"I thought your name was Ray?" Jack said.

"Ray is short for Rainer."

"I can't read the other words. Is it Latin?" I asked.

"Oh, no," Mr. Krum said. "German."

"Why is it in German?"

"What other language would a German medal have on it?"

"German medal? Why would you get a medal from the Germans?" I gasped.

"I was in the German army."

"But I don't understand," I stammered.

"I was born and raised in Germany. My father is German, while my mother is English."

"You're German?" I questioned.

"No," he said, shaking his head.

"But you fought for them in the war."

"Yes, I did. I was born in Germany. *Then* I was German. *Now* I am Canadian. I have lived in Canada since after the war. I've lived right here in Whitby for almost twenty years. I still have a little accent, no?"

"Just a bit," I said.

"It was a different war at a different time for different reasons. I have chosen to become Canadian. I am a citizen and proud of my country of choice. Probably as your father is."

"Our father?" Jack asked.

"Your last name is Braun. That makes you of German heritage too, does it not?" Mr. Krum asked.

"Yeah . . . our Opa, I mean our grandfather, came from Germany," I explained.

"But we're Canadian!" Jack quickly added. "And so is our father!"

"As am I." Mr. Krum took the medal from my hand and placed it back in the case.

"I would not show this to many people. They would not

understand," he said as he gently closed the lid. "They hear or see a German name and they don't understand."

Jack snorted. "We've met people like that."

I lowered my eyes to the floor. We hadn't come across anybody like that until we moved here. Some of the boys in the neighbourhood had been calling me names—although never when Jack was around.

"I . . . we . . . we just didn't know you were from Germany," Jack stammered.

"Many people here are of German descent. For example, our chief of police."

"Chief Smith?"

"I am not the only one to use a slightly different name," Mr. Krum said. "Smith is how the English say the name Schmidt. His real name is Schmidt."

Of course I knew the Chief—or at least knew who he was. He was always driving around in his police car, looking at everything and everybody. He wasn't very friendly, and I was actually afraid of him.

"Some people, when they come to a country, try to hide their roots. This might be wise, I think, especially at a time like this. Some feel that those of us who have German roots are not trustworthy, or at best that we might have mixed allegiance."

Neither Jack nor I said anything, but our expressions left little doubt that we'd worried people might think the same of us.

"Words are useless to convince others of one's loyalty," Mr. Krum said. "As they say, the first casualty of war is the truth. You must look at a man's actions as well as listen to his words." There was a long pause. "Take your father. His actions are to serve his country. Could there be any doubt of his loyalty?"

"None," Jack snapped.

"And I would have done the same, if allowed."

"You were willing to fight against Germany?"

"Against the Nazis," he said, nodding his head enthusiastically. "Do you know what the Nazis did as soon as they came to power? They closed down the newspapers. Their policies, their lies, could not stand the light of truth. They are evil. Fighting against evil is always the right decision. Even if that decision put me at odds with the place of my birth."

A long silence followed. Nobody seemed to know what to say.

"Thanks for showing me your medals," I finally offered, breaking the tension.

"Thank you, George," he said, bowing his head slightly.

"You know what, Mr. Krum," I said, "I think they should have let you join the army."

"You do?"

"Yep. I know you would have been a hero again."

# CHAPTER SEVEN

I THREW THE NEWSPAPER and it flew through the air, hitting the railing of the porch and bouncing back and down into the flowerbed.

"Nice throw," Jack said, sarcastically. It was the first thing he'd said since we'd left the newspaper office.

I walked across the lawn, reached into the bed and retrieved the paper. I tossed it over the railing and it thumped against the front door. Back on the sidewalk Jack was waiting, the heavy bag filled with newspapers slung over his shoulder.

"What's eating you?" I asked.

"Nothing. Just thinking, that's all."

We continued to walk along, tossing papers onto the porches or stairs of his customers.

"That was lucky that we talked to Mr. Krum today."

"Maybe. Maybe not."

"What do you mean? He gave us a lot of information."

"Maybe. Maybe not."

"Is that all you can say?" I asked.

"Maybe. . . . Maybe not," he said with a smirk.

"At least now we know that it's some sort of military base."

"He said it was *probably* a military base," Jack corrected me.

"And you think he's wrong?"

"I *don't* think he's wrong. I just think that there are things he doesn't know about."

"Things like what?"

"Things like those men speaking German, and what we saw on the bridge."

"Maybe we could tell Mr. Krum," I suggested.

Jack grabbed me by the arm and jerked me around to face him. "We can tell him nothing. Understand?"

"Sure . . . I guess. But why not?"

"First, we shouldn't be saying anything to anybody, and second, you know what the poster says, 'Loose Lips Sink Ships.'"

"What does us telling him have to do with boats sinking?"

"It doesn't have anything to do with boats sinking." Jack shook his head in disgust. "It has to do with information and spreading secrets."

"But who is Mr. Krum going to tell?" I asked.

"I don't know . . . you can never be sure," my brother said. "Spies could be anywhere."

"You think Mr. Krum is a spy?" I demanded.

Jack didn't answer. Instead he tossed another paper onto a porch.

"I don't really know what I'm saying," he finally confessed. "I'm confused."

"Just because he has a German last name doesn't mean anything, you know," I pointed out.

"It doesn't mean anything that *we* have a German last name, but him we don't know about," Jack said. "He even fought for Germany in the last war."

"That was before. He's Canadian now. He wanted to fight against the Nazis but they wouldn't let him because he was too old."

"That's what he said."

"What do you mean?" I asked.

"Maybe he *didn't* try to join the army, or maybe he tried but they wouldn't let him in for other reasons. Maybe they wondered if he was a spy," Jack suggested. "Being an editor of the newspaper would be the perfect cover. He said that himself."

"But if he is a spy, why would he tell us that he *could* be a spy? Wouldn't that be the last thing in the world he'd say?" I reasoned.

"Maybe it would be the perfect thing to say. If he says he *could* be a spy, then nobody would believe that he *is* one. Doesn't that make sense?"

"But how about showing us the medals? If he hadn't done that, we wouldn't have even known he was German," I argued.

"Other people in the community already know, I bet, so that really wasn't anything one way or another."

"You don't really believe that, do you?" I asked.

"I don't know what to believe," Jack admitted.

"I think Mr. Krum was just trying to be helpful and nice. He's a nice man. He told us things about the land and explosions and stuff."

"He told us things that would make us stop snooping around that camp."

"But if he was a German spy, wouldn't he *want* us to snoop around the camp?" I asked. "You know, find out things and report back to him?"

Jack dug into his bag, grabbed another paper and flung it up onto the porch of a house.

"Well . . . I guess you're right . . . unless . . ."

"Unless what?"

"Unless that isn't really a Canadian military base."

"What else could it be?"

"Maybe it's a secret base training German spies right here under our noses, and he doesn't want us there because he's afraid we'll expose it."

"Come on, Jack, that's got to be the stupidest thing you've ever said in your whole life!"

"I don't know . . . I just don't know."

"Because if you really believe that, we have to tell somebody . . . Mom or the RCMP or somebody."

"Tell them what?"

"What we've seen and heard," I said.

"We haven't seen or heard enough . . . yet."

I felt my stomach drop down to my knees. "Mr. Krum said we shouldn't go back."

"What else would he say?" Jack asked. "He doesn't want us to go there, and that's one more reason why we are going back . . . tonight."

"You can't be serious."

"I couldn't be more serious," he said. "As soon as Mom goes off to the bus we'll eat and then head into the property. We'll come in the same way, by the creek."

"Jack, I don't want to do that."

"Who said I was even inviting you to join me!" he snapped.

"But you can't go without me!" I protested.

"I can . . . but I won't. If you want to come you're welcome to come with me. Are you in?" he asked.

"I'm in," I said through clenched teeth, against my better judgment.

"Good," he replied. "Now take this." He pulled the newspaper bag off his shoulder and handed it to me.

I took it and gave him a questioning look.

"I'm going to take some papers and cut through to the next street. You keep delivering along here and I'll meet you at the corner. Okay?"

"Sure."

Jack reached into the bag and started to pull out papers. He grabbed six, tucking them under one arm.

"Do you remember all the houses on this block?" he asked.

"Yeah."

"Tell me the numbers."

"I don't know the numbers, I just know the houses."

"Sure you do," he chuckled. "You know the houses *really* well."

"Shut up, Jack, or you can deliver your own papers."

He held up his hands as if he was going to surrender. "Watch out for that dog at one-seventy. Don't even go on the property unless he's tied up."

"I won't," I promised.

"Good. See you in a few minutes."

Jack started down the cross street and I moved on confidently. Imagine him thinking that I couldn't remember which houses he delivered to . . . although they did look pretty much the same . . . and some of them didn't even have numbers yet. Maybe this wasn't going to be as easy as I thought.

I tried to remember which houses were which. I knew he delivered fifteen papers in this section—ten on this side and five on the other. I knew the houses on the other side a lot better because I usually delivered those for him. Maybe I should do the side I knew first and then come back and do this one . . . no, if I did that Jack would be finished first and he'd know I didn't know what I was doing. I'd just have to concentrate.

I looked at the first house on the street, which of course looked like the second and the third. I knew I wasn't delivering to any of those, though. The first house on Jack's route was partway down the block and—I recognized the curtains. I took a newspaper from the bag and whipped it up at the house. It hit the front door with a loud bang. Right house, and good throw. I could do this.

I pitched a paper at the next house. It was a little wide of the door, but close enough for them to see. The next house got a paper as well. I threw that one underhand and it skittered up the walkway and bumped into the front step. The next houses were across the street. I crossed over and delivered another paper.

"Hey, paper boy!"

I jumped slightly into the air and spun around at the sound of the voice. There were three kids walking down the driveway of one of the houses I'd just passed. They looked about my age . . . maybe a little bit older.

"Wait up!" one of them called.

I stood there waiting as they came toward me. There was something about them that made me nervous. Maybe it was the way they were walking, or the look on their faces, but something didn't seem right. They stopped right in front of me.

"Got any extra papers you don't need?" one of them asked.

I shook my head.

"Come on, that bag looks pretty full," another of them tried.

"I . . . need them all," I stammered.

"That seems pretty greedy, not sharing. You gotta have one extra paper. Here, let me have a look."

Before I could even react he grabbed the bag and started to pull it off my shoulder.

"Don't do that!" I practically shouted as I gripped the bag with both hands.

A second kid grabbed it as well and they ripped it from me.

"Give it back!" I pleaded.

"Shut up or we'll do more than just take a paper away from you!" the biggest one threatened.

I shut my mouth and stared down at the sidewalk.

"You don't mind if we take one paper each, do you?" he asked.

I didn't answer.

He reached out and poked me in the shoulder. "You don't mind, do you?" he asked again.

"I hope you don't mind this!"

I looked up at the sound of Jack's voice and saw him smack the biggest kid right in the side of the face! He went down like he'd been shot, and his nose practically exploded. Blood was spurting out and onto the sidewalk.

"My nose! My nose!" he screamed. He'd dropped the newspaper bag and was clutching his face with both hands, like he was afraid his nose was going to drop off.

Jack bent down, grabbed the bag and handed it to me in one quick motion.

"And do either of you mind what I just did?" Jack yelled.

The other two started to back away. They looked shocked and scared and confused all at once. Jack stepped forward. He was big for fourteen, and strong, from working with our father on the farm. He was going to take them both on, right there and then, and I knew that they didn't have a chance.

Everybody back home knew Jack, and knew that I was his brother. These three boys were going to find out why nobody ever bothered us.

"So you think it's funny to pick on somebody when you've got him outnumbered three to one, huh? How about the two of you against me? How about it?" Jack yelled.

"We didn't mean nothing," one of them stammered. "Nothing."

It looked as if they were going to turn and run and—suddenly a car squealed to a stop at the curb. It was a police car! Inside was Chief Smith!

"What's going on here!" he demanded as he climbed out.

Nobody answered.

The Chief lumbered toward us. He was a big man—tall and heavy—and in his uniform, with a gun strapped to his side, he loomed even larger.

"I know you three," he said, pointing to the boys. "What have you been up to?"

"We didn't do nothing!" one of them protested.

The largest of the three staggered to his feet. "He hit me!" he cried, pointing at my brother while still clutching his nose with the other hand. Blood continued to flow through his fingers.

Jack was going to be in trouble now. Maybe I could explain how he had to do it because—

"If he did hit you, then you probably deserved it!" Chief Smith said.

I couldn't believe my ears.

He turned to my brother and me. "Were these three bothering you boys?"

"They were trying to—"

"They weren't doing anything," my brother said, cutting me off. "At least, nothing that we need any help with. We're okay."

The Chief snorted. "It looks like things were going okay. You three, beat it!" he bellowed.

"But he hit me!"

"Get out of here before I hit you too!" the Chief roared.

The three boys didn't need to be told again. They all turned and scampered away.

"I don't know you boys," Chief Smith said.

"We haven't lived here that long," Jack explained.

"Long enough to get a job delivering papers. Where do you live?"

"Chambers Avenue . . . one-ninety," I answered.

"And your names?"

This was the second time in two days that somebody in a uniform had asked us the exact same questions.

"I'm Jack Braun, and this is my brother George."

"Braun?" he said nodding his head. "The name is German, but you two don't look German."

People often told us that because they expected Germans to have blond hair and blue eyes. Our hair was sandy brown, and we had our mother's dark eyes.

"That's because we're not German," Jack said. "We're Canadian."

"I meant your heritage," Chief Smith said. "Don't take offence. I'm of German blood too."

"We know," I said.

"Do you?" His voice became deeper and his brow furrowed. "And how would you know that?"

"Well . . . Mr. Krum told us," I explained.

He smiled, and I suddenly felt better. "Those boys weren't bothering you because you have a German name, were they?"

"They don't even know our name," I said.

"Good, because nobody is going to be doing that in my town. Anybody bothers you, then you let me know, okay?"

"Thanks," I said.

"You're welcome. Now, do you boys need a ride home?" he asked.

Jack shook his head. "We have to finish my paper route."

"I'll let you get on your way then. I don't think those boys will be bothering you again today."

"That's too bad," my brother said.

The Chief looked a little bit shocked and then smiled. "If those three boys are half smart—and that might be a stretch—they'll never bother the two of you again. I'll see you boys around. And remember . . . us Krauts have to stick together."

Chief Smith walked back to his car as we started back down the street. He passed by, honked his horn and waved. I waved back.

"He seems like a nice guy," I said, feeling relieved.

"You think everybody's a nice guy," Jack replied.

"Not everybody. Not those kids."

"Besides those kids. You think Mr. Krum is a nice guy, and Chief Smith is a nice guy."

"They seem nice to me," I answered with a shrug.

"They both make me nervous," Jack said. "And what did he mean 'us Krauts have to stick together'?"

"I think he was just making a joke."

"It wasn't funny," Jack muttered. "And another thing . . . the next time somebody bothers you, just pop 'em in the nose. I can't be around to rescue you your whole life."

# CHAPTER EIGHT

WE DRIFTED AROUND ANOTHER bend in the creek, and up ahead I could see the railroad trestle. It was deserted. No people in black clothing. No train. Just up ahead and off to the side was the large willow tree that had given us shelter before. I wanted shelter—the shelter of my house. I wanted to turn around. I wanted to go home, climb into my bed and pull up the covers. I wasn't going to get anything that I wanted.

I'd spent a good part of the day trying to convince Jack that we shouldn't be doing this. He hadn't even bothered to argue back. He'd just told me that I was a "sucky baby" and he didn't even want me to come along anyway. Finally he'd told me that if I said another word he'd just "clean my clock" worse than he'd done to that kid. That was the end of the discussion. I'd seen Jack in enough fights to know I didn't ever want to get in a serious one with him. Actually, I didn't want to fight Jack or anybody else.

The creek dipped and my stomach flipped. I paddled with my hands so I could manoeuvre the inner tube through the centre support of the bridge. It dipped again and the tube started to spin around, but I was able to stay in control and send it shooting through the right spot. Jack was right beside me.

I paddled hard again, sending the tube out of the current and into the little eddy where we'd beached the tubes the last time. Once we were into the shallow water I jumped off. At least I didn't have to worry about what was underfoot. I was wearing my sneakers. Jack and I had agreed to wear shoes this time. We waded out of the water and onto the bank.

"Right here," Jack said, putting his tube underneath a bush.

I put mine in beside it, far enough from the shore to guarantee there was no way it was going to drift away this time.

Without a word Jack started off, and I fell in behind him. There really wasn't much to say, and besides, the quieter we were the better the chance that we wouldn't be seen.

I didn't have my watch with me—I didn't want to risk ruining it on the creek ride—but I really wanted to know the time. The only thing I'd got Jack to agree to was that we'd head back in time to be home before dark. I figured it had to be close to five-thirty already.

"This way," Jack said.

I followed him through the wire fence again and then across the field and into the trees. I figured he had a pretty good idea where we were headed, but that didn't stop me from keeping one eye on the railroad embankment. As long as it was in sight I knew where we were and, more important, how to get home.

"Let's stop and get a drink," Jack suggested.

I cupped my hands and scooped a small slurp of water from the stream that trickled through the bush. Jack did the same. Of course I knew where we were now. This was just up from the spot where we'd hidden and watched those men being taken prisoner . . . or pretending to be taken prisoner . . . or whatever it was that we saw.

"Which way are we going?" I asked.

"That way. We'll walk on the edge of the field, close to the scrub and trees."

"Wouldn't it be safer to stay hidden?"

"It'll take too long. We'll be okay as long as we move slowly and listen. As soon as we hear the sound of a jeep we can get into the bush before anyone sees us."

Jack stumbled over the rocks and pushed through the brush to reach the edge of the field. I followed. Looking beyond him, I could see the land sloping gently down and away from us. It was bordered on the far side—it had to be at least a hundred yards away—by a line of trees and brush. Maybe there was another field on the other side.

We moved around the perimeter. The only sounds we could hear were the birds chirping from the surrounding forest. It was easy to forget that we weren't just out for a friendly stroll. Actually, so much of what we'd seen was so unreal that it would have been easier just to think that none of it had even happened. Maybe it was like a strange dream, or a book that I'd read and partly forgotten. Or maybe I'd just imagined the whole thing in the first place!

"It's pretty here," I said.

"What?"

"It's pretty."

"I guess. I hadn't thought about that." Jack stopped. "You hear anything?"

I halted in my tracks. What had he heard?

"Do *you* hear something?" I asked anxiously.

"I thought I heard voices . . . that way," he said, pointing into the trees. "Do you hear it?"

I pricked up my ears. "Maybe . . . something."

"Come on." Jack changed course to head into the woods.

Part of me was grateful to be out of the open and heading back into cover. The other part thought it was plain crazy to be heading *toward* voices. We should have been going in the opposite direction. Besides, maybe those weren't even voices. And if they were, the way the wind was blowing, they could have been coming from anywhere.

"Holy . . ."

I was grabbed and pushed down to the ground by Jack.

"Did you see that!" I gasped.

"Of course I did. Why do you think I knocked you down?"

Just on the other side of the trees there was another field, and in the middle of the field were jeeps and a dozen or more men and a tower—a tower that must have been more than a hundred feet high!

"We've got to get away from here!" I hissed.

"What are they doing?" Jack wondered out loud.

"I don't care what they're doing . . . I just want to get out of here!"

"We're not going anywhere until I figure out what's happening," Jack said.

I just closed my mouth.

"Maybe it's an observation tower. There are people climbing up the side."

Jack was right. There were four or five men climbing up a series of sets of stairs that led to the top of the tower.

"What are they hoping to see, Jack?"

"Maybe people trying to sneak in . . . like us."

I involuntarily pressed myself closer to the ground.

"They don't look like Germans," I said.

"All I can say for sure is that they aren't wearing German uniforms. But then, they're not wearing *any* uniforms."

"They're all sort of dressed the same," I noted. All of the men were in greenish-grey pants and shirts and wore similar-looking boots.

"And the jeeps. You notice that they don't have any writing on them, or even numbers and letters, like a serial number or—"

"Oh my gosh!"

As we watched, a man jumped from the tower and a parachute opened up over top of him. He drifted down and away from the tower and then landed, rolling until the chute closed in around him. A number of the men on the ground ran over and helped unravel him and remove the parachute.

He was hardly out of his chute before a second man leaped off the tower. His chute opened and he drifted down, hitting the ground at almost the same spot as the first man. But instead of tumbling he stayed on his feet, running forward. He grabbed the parachute and rapidly gathered it in his arms until he was carrying it.

"That's amazing," Jack said. "I'd love to try that."

"Not me, I like to have both my feet on the—"

I stopped at the sound of an engine. I looked up. A small airplane was visible on the horizon. As I watched, it came lower and lower. Its engine whined as it passed directly over our heads. It banked to the side and then came back for another pass.

"What is it doing?" I said, more to myself than to Jack.

"I think it's going to land."

"Here in the field?"

"I think so."

It came over once more, so low now that I could make out the faces on the people through the side window. It was a small plane, one engine, no markings and black in colour . . . totally black.

"It's coming down," Jack said.

The wheels of the little plane practically brushed the tops of the trees to the left as it came in for a landing. When the wheels hit the grass it bounced ever so slightly, touching down again and rolling up the grassy field. As it started to slow down, a jeep went racing toward it. The plane came to a stop just as the jeep got to its side. A door popped open and a man jumped out. As he ran for the jeep the whine of the airplane engine became louder and the plane started into motion again. It taxied to the end of the field and then spun around. The plane began picking up speed, faster and faster. It looked as though the pilot was taking off again.

"Those trees are awfully close," I said. "Do you think he'll make it?"

"He'll make it just fine," a voice called out from behind us, and a chill shot through my entire body.

Slowly Jack and I turned around. There were four soldiers standing right behind us, rifles at the ready! I recognized one of them from the other night.

"You boys are going to regret not listening to me when I told you never to come back here," he said.

# CHAPTER NINE

BEFORE I COULD REACT I was grabbed and hauled to my feet by two of the soldiers. They gripped me so tightly I wanted to scream out in pain, but I was too scared even to make a noise. My feet barely touched the ground as they carried me out of the brush and into the field.

"Let me go!" Jack shouted.

I turned partway around. My brother was struggling against two other soldiers, who were pushing and dragging him out into the open.

Up ahead there were dozens and dozens of men—the men we'd been staring at. But now all eyes were on us. Desperately I wanted to get away, run or hide or—they held me in their steely grip, it was no use even trying to struggle. I was trapped. I felt like a pig being herded into the back of a truck to be sent to the slaughterhouse.

"Where are you taking us?" Jack demanded.

There was no answer. I tried as hard as I could not to cry.

"Where are you taking us?" Jack called out again.

"Shut up!" one of the men barked. "Just shut right up, kid!"

A jeep roared toward us and then squealed to a stop. Jack was thrown into the back seat, and I was lifted off the ground and tossed almost on top of him. One of the men, the one from before, climbed into the empty front seat. He looked back at us, and his expression was frightening. I pressed myself back into the seat to try and get just a little bit farther away from him.

Two of the others climbed up on the back of the jeep so they were standing above us, holding onto the roll bar.

"Where to?" the driver asked.

"The farmhouse," the man in the passenger seat instructed.

The driver nodded, and then the gears of the jeep ground together noisily and it jerked forward, throwing me back against the seat. We circled around the tower. If I had been frightened during that first ride, I was completely terrified this time.

I couldn't help but look at the scene around me. There were still men climbing up the wooden structure, and a dozen more sitting at the base in front of another man—it reminded me of the way my class would sit in front of our teacher. As we moved beyond it I turned slightly around to keep looking and—

"Turn back around! You've seen too much already, haven't you now!" the man in the front seat barked.

My head snapped back around and I fixed my eyes on the floor. I felt my entire body start to shake and I bit down on the inside of my cheek to stop myself from crying. I didn't want to cry . . . I wasn't a baby.

The jeep hit a bump and I was bounced into the air. Jack reached out and grabbed me by the leg and pulled me down. I looked over.

"I'm here," he mouthed over the roar of the jeep.

Of course I knew he was, but somehow him saying that helped stop some of the shaking in my legs. Jack was always there for me. Just like with those kids. Jack always said that nobody was allowed to pick on his baby brother. Nobody but him.

We quickly left the field and bounced onto a dirt road. Was this the track from the other night? Maybe they were just going to drop us off again and—and then I remembered he'd said something about a farmhouse. The jeep began to pick up speed.

Off in the distance I could see the lake, dark and ominous. And up ahead the large antenna rose to the clouds, practically scraping the sky. It was getting bigger and bigger as we closed in. I guessed I'd have things I could say to Mr. Krum now . . . assuming I'd still be alive to say anything to anybody. What were they going to do with us? I didn't even know who these men were . . . but they had to be soldiers . . . didn't they? And did that make it better? What was going to happen?

The vehicle slowed down and turned onto another, larger road that led straight into a forest of chestnut trees. We burst through the woods and suddenly there were buildings all around us. Straight ahead sat an old house, and a big barn, and five or six other buildings that looked newly erected. They were large and long and flat. Was this where that truck Mr. Krum had followed delivered its lumber? The jeep came to a stop directly in front of the house . . . an old farmhouse. This was where they were taking us.

"Out!" the man in the front ordered.

Jack and I climbed out of the jeep. My legs were so shaky that I stumbled until I was caught by powerful hands, steadied and then released. Instinctively I looked around, trying to figure out if there was any place to run. In that split second that I hesitated I was shoved from behind and almost tumbled over again.

"Get moving!"

Jack and I fell in behind the one man, and the two soldiers walked right behind us. I chanced a glance over my shoulder and was shocked to see that they weren't just following behind but held their rifles in front of them!

I tripped up the front stairs of the farmhouse, the sounds of the soldiers' boots thundering against the wooden floor of the porch behind me. My own feet, clad in my soaked sneakers, were silent.

The soldier in the lead opened the front door. I didn't want to go in there . . . I had to get away. I stopped and was again shoved from behind, propelled through the open door.

I was now standing in a kitchen—or what should have been the kitchen. There were cupboards and a sink, but no stove or fridge or table. There were chairs against the wall on one side of the room, and a large chalkboard had been attached to the opposite wall.

"Sit!" the man barked, and Jack and I took two of the chairs.

"Guard them," he said, and he turned and left the room.

The two soldiers came over and stood right over top of us.

"It's going to be okay," Jack said to me quietly.

"Hah!" one of the men exclaimed. "That's where you're wrong, that's where you're *dead* wrong!"

The shaky feeling in my legs got worse and my whole body started to tremble. I tried to stop it, but I couldn't. My chin began shaking and my tongue felt thick and I couldn't hold back any more. I started to bawl. I knew I shouldn't have, but I couldn't control it. Jack would be mad at me for acting like a baby.

"Both of you, up!" barked the man, who had reappeared at the doorway.

I staggered to my feet. One of the soldiers grabbed me by the arm and steadied me. We followed him down a hall to a closed door. He knocked.

"Come!" came a voice through the door.

The soldier opened it and entered. Jack went next and I followed behind. There was a man, an older man, seated behind a large desk. He had a moustache and wore a plain white shirt. In front of the desk were two chairs.

"Sit, gentlemen," he said, gesturing to the empty seats.

Jack and I sat down. I was happy just to be sitting because it didn't feel like my legs could hold me up much longer.

"You're dismissed," he said.

"Yes, sir." Our escort left, closing the door behind him.

Whoever this man was, he was in charge. My eyes had been fixed on the floor, but now I chanced a look at him. He wasn't looking at us. He was studying some papers inside a brown file folder. He looked up and caught me looking at him and I instantly looked down again.

"What do you have to say for yourselves?" the man asked.

"We're . . . we're . . . not afraid of you," Jack stammered.

The man chuckled. "That is a most peculiar statement. Your brother seems to be rather scared, unless I misread those for tears of joy he's experiencing."

Jack shot me a nasty look that said "Stop your blubbering," but I knew I couldn't.

"I think if I were in your position I would be terrified," the man went on.

"We're not!" Jack snapped. "And you'd better let us go or you're in *big* trouble!"

"I certainly wouldn't want to be in *big* trouble," the man said. "And just who would cause us that trouble?"

"The police, or maybe even the army!" Jack said.

The man suddenly started to laugh. That unnerved me more then being yelled at. He closed the file, stood up and circled around his desk until he stood right in front of us. He then perched on the edge.

"And who exactly do you think we are?" he asked.

"Um . . . we're . . . we're not really sure," I answered uncertainly.

"This is a restricted military base," he stated sternly. "We *are* the army."

I swallowed hard and started to cry even louder.

"There's nothing to cry about, George."

I looked up at him, wide-eyed.

"How do you know his name?" Jack demanded.

"I know both your names, Jack, and much, much more."

He reached back, grabbed the big folder off his desk and opened it again.

"You are Jack Braun and you certainly are very brave. You are rather a big lad for only fourteen years of age. I would have thought you to be older. And George is twelve in a few more days. May I offer you an early birthday greeting?"

"Thanks," I sniffled, trying again to put away the tears.

"Your mother's name is Christina, although she prefers the name Betty. She is employed at the Defence Industries plant, working on the line. Am I to assume that she is working the swing shift this evening?"

I nodded my head.

"That would explain the two of you being here instead of safely at home getting ready to be tucked into bed." He turned his eyes back to the file folder. "Your father is serving with the St. Patrick's Regiment. He volunteered for service and is presently stationed in Africa."

"You know about our dad?" Jack asked.

"I know everything about you two. It's all right here," he said, tapping the folder with a finger.

"But how?"

"We are in the business of gathering information. A file is opened on all persons who come to our attention, as you did the other night when you tried to enter our camp. There isn't much that we can't find out, although I have one question that remains unanswered."

"What's that?" Jack asked.

"Why did you gentlemen return here again?"

"Well . . . we sort of had to," Jack said under his breath.

"Had to?"

Jack looked down at the ground. "We sort of thought that maybe there were Nazi agents here," he mumbled.

"And just why would you think that?"

"Because we heard men speaking German," Jack said.

"You heard people speaking German today?"

"Not today."

"The time you were detained?"

"Sort of another time we were here," he answered reluctantly.

"How many times have you been here?"

"Just three times," Jack said. "And the first two times were by accident."

"We wouldn't have come again at all if we hadn't seen those men on the bridge," I blurted out.

"Men on the bridge?"

"They were all dressed in black, and they had wires, and we thought they were trying to blow up the bridge," I tried to explain.

"Oh my Lord," he said as he rose to his feet. "You saw people on the bridge."

"And then we heard them speaking German when they

were captured, or I guess not really captured, by the men in the jeep," Jack added.

"And this all took place by the bridge?"

"Not really. We followed them in and then they didn't see us."

"You followed some of our men and they didn't notice?" he asked in disbelief.

"There were four of them," I said. "And we didn't exactly follow right behind them, but we were close to them. That's when we heard them speaking German, and the men in the jeep with the guns were speaking German, and then we started to think that everybody was German!"

"This is most distressing . . . most," he said, shaking his head. "Is there anything else you've seen that I should be made aware of?"

"I don't think so," Jack said. "Unless you include the airplane landing."

"And that tower," I added. "The place where everybody was jumping off that tower with their parachutes."

"And the big antenna," Jack said. "We saw it, but we don't know what it's for."

"I suppose I should at least be grateful that you weren't too close to the demolition exercises." He paused. "You didn't see us blowing anything up, did you?"

Jack shook his head.

"We just heard about that from Mr. Krum," I explained.

"Rainer Krum, the editor of the Whitby newspaper?"

I nodded my head.

"And what brought you to seek out Mr. Krum?"

"We didn't really go looking for him. We were just sort of talking when we were sorting through my papers," Jack said. "And he heard us talking."

"About this camp?"

"Sort of, but not really," I told him. "We were talking about spies and stuff and he heard us."

"And did you talk to him about what you'd seen here?"

Jack shook his head. "We didn't talk. We listened."

The man nodded his head approvingly. "A lesson, it would seem, that my men would be wise to learn."

"And we agreed that we're not going to talk to him again, anyway," Jack said.

"And why is that?"

Jack suddenly looked embarrassed. "I just thought that maybe he could be a German spy too."

"It appears that you two boys think that *everybody* is a German spy."

"But he *is* German. He even showed us his medals!" I said, defending Jack.

"Yes. He was quite the hero for the Germans in the First World War."

"You know about that?" I asked, and then I thought things through a little further. Of course he knew about Mr. Krum. "You have a file on him too, don't you?"

"Why would you think that?"

"You said you open files on everybody who comes to your attention like we did, and he was stopped once too, so I thought there'd be a file," I explained.

"You are resourceful young men. But I would prefer that you didn't discuss any of this with Mr. Krum."

"We won't talk to anybody about anything . . ." I paused. Why did he mention not talking to Mr. Krum instead of not talking to anybody?

"You don't think Mr. Krum is a . . . is a spy, do you?" I asked.

Now it was his turn to pause before talking. "George, if we thought Mr. Krum was a spy, don't you think we would have arrested him?"

"Well, sure, of course," I stammered.

"We wouldn't just let a known spy wander around, now, would we?" he continued. "It is just that he is the editor of the local paper, and I wouldn't want him to become aware of this and possibly write a story."

"But wouldn't you just censor anything that he tried to write about the camp?" I asked.

"Why yes, we could, but it's better that he simply not be aware of things and . . . how is it that you know about censoring stories?"

"Mr. Krum told us about it," Jack answered.

"He seems to have told you a great deal. And it is important that neither Mr. Krum, nor anybody else, finds out anything from you. Do you boys realize what you have done?"

"No, sir," Jack said, shaking his head.

"You have somehow managed to penetrate what is supposed to be a highly restricted, highly secure military facility. And in doing so you have learned far, far more than I would have imagined."

"We won't tell anybody anything," Jack said. "I promise."

"We won't . . . honestly," I added. "We just want to go home now."

"I am afraid that I will not be allowing you gentlemen to leave at this time."

"But we have to! Our mother is going to call us on her break and she'll be worried if we're not home."

"You won't be home for that call. You have left me with no choice."

# CHAPTER TEN

"STAY HERE." THE MAN in charge stood up, and left the room, closing the door behind him. We were alone.

"Jack . . . what did he mean . . . what's going to happen?" I asked, my voice quavering. I thought I was going to start to cry again.

"I don't know," Jack answered anxiously.

"He can't keep us . . . can he?"

"I don't know."

"But they're on our side . . . we're on their side . . . aren't we?" I cried.

"I don't know! Now stop crying and let me think. We got to get out of here," Jack snapped. He jumped to his feet and raced over to the window, and I got up to join him. A thick white blind let in light but blocked the view.

Jack pulled the blind away so we could both peer outside. There was a jeep visible just in front of us. Behind that was a large building. It was long and flat and one storey high. It not only looked newly built, but it seemed out of place on a farm. There were four other, much smaller buildings. They looked new as well. In the distance three men exited one of the buildings and walked away, disappearing around the corner.

Jack fumbled with the latch at the top of the window. "It's jammed!" he hissed. "I can't get it open!"

"Maybe we can smash it!" I said.

"Too noisy, somebody will hear. I'll just try harder and then—"

"Are you boys plotting a daring escape?"

We both jumped into the air and spun around in shock. It was the man who had just interrogated us. He'd come back.

"We were looking, that's all," I said.

"I would think that you two have seen far too much already. Please take your seats again."

Jack let go of the blind and it fell back into place, blocking the outside world from view. Slowly he started back to his seat. I followed, eyeing the door as I walked—maybe I could make a dash for it and get away.

"Hurry up, gentlemen," he said as he again took up a perch on the edge of his desk. He had some papers in his hands, and as he studied them we remained silent.

Strangely, it reminded me of the time when I was called before the school principal for throwing snowballs and I had to wait to hear what he was going to do to me. It seemed silly now, thinking back, how scared I'd been. What was the worst thing the principal could have done? A shudder suddenly ran through my entire body as I tried to imagine the worst thing this man could do . . . I couldn't even let that enter my mind.

"As you boys are acutely aware," he said, "this country is at war. And as a result the government has many very special powers. Any citizen of this country can be asked, at a moment's notice, to do service for his or her country. Were you aware of that?"

I shook my head.

"And that service cannot be denied, regardless of circumstances. I am requesting that you both read this document," he said, handing a piece of paper to each of us. "And upon reading I will ask that you both affix your signature at the bottom."

"What is it?" Jack asked.

"I am asking you to sign an oath under the Official Secrets Act."

"I don't understand," I said.

"You are signing an oath stating that as agents of this government you will not divulge anything to anybody about what you have learned."

"Agents of the government . . . what does that mean?"

"It means that you are officially being enlisted into the service of your country."

"You mean like soldiers?" Jack asked.

"Or like spies?" I suggested.

"Spies . . . why would you say that?" he asked.

"I was just thinking. This isn't a regular army base, is it? This is some sort of special camp . . . right?"

He smiled. "I'm afraid I can't answer that question. I still need you boys to sign the oath."

"We won't tell anybody, honestly!" Jack said.

"I am *insisting* on your silence. Punishment for violating this oath is imprisonment or, in extreme cases, execution."

"Execution?" I gasped. "Like killing somebody?"

"A firing squad is customary in military matters. You must sign this oath being fully aware of the possible consequences of your actions. Do you understand and agree to these terms?"

"You can count on us," I said.

"We won't tell anybody," Jack agreed. "Even if we're tortured by Nazi agents."

"Hopefully that will not present itself as a reality."

"And can we go home after we sign?" I asked. "We have to be there before—"

"You don't have to worry about your mother calling at break," he said.

"But she calls every night," Jack tried to explain.

"Not tonight. All of the phones are going to be, shall we say, unavailable for use."

"How do you know that?"

"That was one of the things I arranged when I was out of the room. The telephones at the D.I.L. plant will be out of order throughout the last break this evening."

"You can do that?" I asked.

He smiled. "We can do many things."

"But if we just signed the oaths we could get home before she calls. There's still time."

"There is still much to be done prior to your leaving this evening," he said. "You will be meeting with one of my men, who will be asking you much the same questions I have asked but in more detail. And your answers will be carefully written down."

"But we told you the truth, honest!" Jack told him.

"I believe you did. But there is much we need to learn from you two boys."

"Learn from us?"

He nodded his head. "We need to know exactly what information you were able to gather, as well as the manner in which you were able to enter this area and leave again. And I am also interested in what Mr. Krum discussed with you, what he is aware of. I would prefer that the editor of the local paper remain in the dark. I'm sure you understand. Now, before I go, does either of you have any questions?"

"Yeah. Are you L.C.?" I asked.

"L.C.? Now how did you know my rank?"

"Your rank?"

"L.C. . . . Lieutenant-Colonel."

"We heard a couple of the soldiers talking about having to meet you," Jack said.

"Being the commander I'm given many nicknames by the men. L.C. is one of the more polite ones. Now, if you gentlemen will excuse me, your appearance has gotten in the way of my work and I still have much to do before the end of this evening."

The car slowed down and then came to a stop. Almost instantly our escort, his name was Bill, opened the door and jumped out. There had been three men in the room during the questioning that the Lieutenant-Colonel had prepared us for, but he had been the one doing most of the talking.

"Time to get out, boys," he said.

"Here?" We were on a deserted stretch of the highway a few blocks from our house.

"Why here?" Jack asked as he climbed out and I followed behind him.

"Orders."

"But I thought you were driving us home."

"This is as close as we go. We can't chance you being seen by your neighbours getting out of a car. It could lead to questions. You have to walk from here."

"Are you sure our mother isn't home yet?" Jack asked.

"By a strange coincidence, her bus broke down on the trip back from the plant. It won't be, shall we say, *fixed,* until the moment you enter your house. And remember that you cannot discuss what happened with anybody, including your mother."

"We know."

"Good. Goodnight."

"Yeah, goodnight," Jack said.

"And thanks for the ride," I added.

Bill nodded. "Thank you for the information. We'll be in touch," he said, and he jumped back into the car.

The door slammed and the car roared off, leaving us in a hail of dust and gravel.

"Did you hear what he said?" I asked Jack.

"Sure . . . he said goodnight . . . and thanked us."

"And said they'd be in touch."

"He was probably just saying that like people say 'take care' or 'have a pleasant night.' It doesn't mean anything."

"I'm not so sure."

"I am. What else could they ask us that they didn't already ask us tonight?"

"Maybe you're right," I admitted.

"I'm always right!" Jack declared.

"Sure you are. So I guess that makes them all German spies, right?"

"Shut up and let's get walking."

The highway was completely deserted, no cars in sight for a long stretch in either direction. We veered off and cut through an empty lot to come out on our street. Most of the houses were dark, but there were a few porch lights on. I wondered if people in those houses were waiting for somebody who was on the same bus that was carrying our mother.

We came up to our house. Our porch light was on too, and for an instant I was afraid that Mom was home until I remembered we'd switched it on before leaving that afternoon. We probably shouldn't have left the light on—it was wasting energy and that could hurt the war effort—but we hadn't wanted to come home to a totally dark house. We circled around and went in through the side door. Jack threw on a light.

"Hello!" he called out.

"Who are you calling?"

"Just making sure Mom's not home yet," Jack answered. "We'd better get into bed, it's incredibly late."

I looked up at the clock above the piano. It was three minutes before two. If I hadn't known where Mom was I would have been worried to death. She was always home by twelve-thirty, or quarter to one at the latest.

Jack and I went to our bedroom and quickly changed into our pajamas. My brother threw his clothes onto the floor and kicked them around with his foot.

"We have to make it look lived in," he said. "We'll just turn out the lights and . . . Supper—we didn't clean up after supper! The kitchen is still a mess! We have to clean it or Mom will kill us!"

We rushed to the kitchen. There were dishes everywhere. We'd figured we'd have plenty of time to clean up sometime between getting home and getting to bed. We hadn't figured on not getting home until two in the morning.

Jack filled up the sink and rubbed the cloth against a small piece of dish soap. I frantically started scraping the plates off and tossing them into the water.

"I'll wash, you dry and put things away," Jack ordered. "Wipe down the counter and the table."

I grabbed a cloth from the sink and started to follow his directions, beginning with the table. I wiped part and then moved dishes to the sink, returning to wipe down another section. Soon both the counter and table were clean, so I took a tea towel and started to dry part of the growing dish pile. We'd never cleaned up so fast. Jack finished scrubbing out the casserole dish—Mom had made us a casserole for supper and all we'd had to do was heat it up. He then took a broom and began to sweep the floor.

"We don't usually sweep up," I said.

He looked at me, then the broom, and shrugged. "You're right. I'll help you finish that up, and then we gotta be in bed before Mom comes through that door or we're dead. She'll have old lady Henderson sitting us starting tomorrow."

Jack hadn't meant that as a threat but it certainly made me move just a little bit faster. Jack had gotten another tea towel and pitched in. Within a minute I was drying the last of the cutlery and dropping it into the drawer.

"Great, now let's get upstairs and—"

The door burst open. "Boys, I'm home!" Mom called out.

We were dead.

Mom rushed over and to my complete shock threw one arm around me and the other around Jack, pulling us close to her. My eyes caught Jack's. He looked as surprised as me.

"I'm so sorry, boys! It wasn't my fault I'm so late. You must be worried sick!"

"We knew there was trouble with the bus," I said.

"You did? How did you know that?"

"Um . . . I . . ." Of course there was no possible way I could have known.

"We figured it *must* be trouble with the bus," Jack said, jumping in to rescue me. "You know how you're always saying how broken down it is?"

"Yes . . . I guess I have mentioned that a couple of times . . ."

"So is that what happened?" Jack asked.

"Yes, but—"

"I told George that was all that happened. He didn't believe me, but I told him not to worry, that you'd be home soon."

"I thought you'd both be frantic," she said.

"Come on, Mom, I'm fourteen and in charge. There was nothing to worry about," Jack reassured her. "I tried to send him to bed, but he was too worried, so that's why we're still up. That's okay, isn't it?"

"That's all right," Mom said. She gave me a little kiss on the cheek and then did the same to Jack. "I thought you'd be worried, especially after I wasn't able to call you on my break like I always do."

"We were so busy cleaning up the kitchen that we didn't even notice you didn't call until later," Jack said. "You know there's nothing to worry about as long as I'm in charge."

"You really are the man of the house," she said, giving him another kiss. "Now, I think it's time that all of us got to bed."

We said our goodnights and then headed for our bedroom. I snuggled down into the sheets while Jack turned off the lights.

"That was a good one," Jack said sarcastically.

"What?"

"About the bus. We'd better hope there are no Nazi spies around here or they won't need to torture you to get the truth."

"It just sort of slipped out," I apologized.

"Just 'cause you're my little brother doesn't mean you have to be my *stupid* little brother."

I wanted to say something to Jack but didn't know if I could. I swallowed hard.

"Jack?"

"What?"

"Thanks . . . thanks for being there and everything."

"Sure. Go to sleep . . . and try not to be so stupid in the future, okay?"

"I'll try. Goodnight."

# CHAPTER ELEVEN

"HOW ARE YOU DOING today, boys?" Mr. Krum asked.

"Good," Jack said.

"Yeah, good. Really good," I added.

We were out on the loading dock at the newspaper offices getting Jack's papers ready to deliver.

"Peter Cook just called in sick. I was wondering if you could deliver an extra route for me today," Mr. Krum asked. "If you do not have anything else to do?"

Jack looked at me. "I guess I could. My brother could help me. He's responsible enough that he could do a route all by himself."

Jack thought I was responsible? Where did that come from?

"How old are you, George?"

"Almost twelve."

"In just a few days," Jack added.

"I usually like my delivery boys to be at least thirteen, but sometimes rules are meant to be broken, especially for a responsible young man."

"Thanks," I said.

"No promises, you understand, and there are no routes available today, but helping today—and you will be paid for your efforts, of course—only works in your favour."

"That's great," Jack said.

"A little extra money could buy an extra treat or two." Mr. Krum smiled.

"We don't buy many treats," Jack told him. "I use most of my money to buy war saving stamps."

"Me too," I said.

The stamps were issued by the government, and people bought them to support the war. Each stamp cost twenty-five cents, and when you saved sixteen of them your book was filled and you traded it in for a certificate. Then in seven years the government would give you five dollars for your certificate.

"Two more stamps and my book will be full," Jack said proudly.

"Very commendable," Mr. Krum said. "It is nice to know that you are not simply wasting your money."

"Do you save stamps?" I asked Mr. Krum.

"Oh, believe me, I am doing my part to make sure the right side wins this war. Now, back to the business at hand. You'll need another newspaper bag and the list of Peter's customers, and you'll have to prepare his papers. Do you know how to do that, George?"

"Sure. No problem." It wasn't difficult. It involved making sure that all the sections were in place, slipping in any advertisement supplements and then folding it so it would hold together when it was thrown.

"Come and we'll get that bag and list."

I followed him back through the loading area, passing by the familiar posters. The one that said "Your Country Needs You!" meant a lot more to me than it had the day before. I was now an "agent" of my country.

"So George, I trust that you and your brother have not been back up to that farm we talked about?"

"No, no we haven't," I said. I felt uncomfortable. Was I breaking the oath by even talking about it?

"That pleases me, but also surprises me. It remains the best mystery around here. I thought you and your brother would be standing on the fence and looking in as far as you could see."

"You told us we shouldn't go."

"I did?"

"Yes, you said we shouldn't go up there, so we didn't."

"I wish everybody would listen to me that well." He handed me a canvas sack.

"Thank you. I'll return it right after I deliver the papers."

"That's all right. You hang onto it. It might not be that long before you will be needing it every day," he added with a smile. "Did you know that many of the finest reporters started out as paper boys? And in some remarkable cases they had their first big break and wrote their first stories for the paper while they were still delivering it. Is that not remarkable?"

"It is," I agreed.

"And that is why it is important always to keep your eyes open. Now here is a copy of Peter's delivery list," he said, pulling it out of his pocket. "His route is smaller than your brother's. He has only eighty-seven papers to deliver."

"That won't take too long."

I followed Mr. Krum back out to where my brother was just finishing up the last of his papers.

"Today you and your brother should work together. Later, if this becomes a regular assignment, that will not be necessary."

That was fine with me. The last thing I wanted was to run into those boys again when Jack wasn't around. I didn't want to rely on the police chief chancing by . . . actually, I didn't want to run into him, either.

"I was talking to your brother about the old Sinclair property. He said you did not have any interest in going out there any more."

Jack looked at me with alarm, and then his expression softened. "We just haven't had any time lately."

"Really? What have you been doing instead?"

"Nothing much . . . swimming in the creek."

"Corbett's Creek?"

"I think that's what it's called," Jack said.

"That is actually the western boundary of the Sinclair property. Did you not know that?" Mr. Krum asked.

"No, I just knew it was a nice place to swim."

"Is the water deep?"

"In some places," Jack said. "Mostly shallow. We like to just float in our inner tubes."

"That would be relaxing. Could I suggest that while you are floating you keep your eyes open?"

"I guess we could," Jack said.

"Excellent. As I was saying to your brother, the best story around these parts is contained within the boundaries of that farm. Of that I am certain."

"If we see anything, we'll let you know about it," Jack agreed.

"Who knows? You might be the ones who break the story."

"But won't they block the story, you know, not let you run it, if it has to do with the army?" I asked.

"You are correct," he said. "They will most likely not allow it to be published. It might simply be something that is shared with me to satisfy my curiosity. As I mentioned, newspapermen are most curious and nosy by nature. So if you hear or see anything, you tell me, and if I find out anything, I will tell you. Agreed?"

"Sure, no problem," Jack told him.

"I guess so."

"There is nothing to guess. We are all members of the same family, the same newspaper family, and we will share information. That is how good newspapermen work. Now I shall get back to the job of running the paper, and you get back to delivering it."

We watched him go back inside, leaving us alone.

I leaned in close to Jack. "You didn't mean any of that, did you?"

"About sharing information?"

I nodded.

"Of course not. Let's not talk about it now. Fold papers."

Jack went inside to get more newspapers and I continued to fold. A couple of the other carriers came out with their bundles. They nodded a greeting and one walked off while the second climbed onto a bike and rode away. Jack returned with his arms full of papers. I wanted to talk so I tried to get mine ready as quickly as I could.

"The money for doing this extra route today will go in my pay packet," Jack said. "You can have all of it."

"I think we should split it. You're coming with me to help deliver."

"And you're coming along with me to deliver my route," he said.

"But I always come with you."

"Yeah, so maybe I should always be giving you a split of my pay."

"Are you serious?" I couldn't believe my ears.

"Not much, but something . . . as long as you don't bug me."

"I guess that means I'll *never* see a cent of it."

Jack flashed me a smile. "There's always a chance you won't bug me . . . at least, not too much."

Trucks pulled up and left, and four more paper boys arrived and started to prepare their bundles. Jack liked to arrive early because sometimes there was a foul-up with the press and there weren't enough papers until later. Mr. Krum appeared at the door of the loading dock, and for a second I thought he was coming out to talk to us, but then he disappeared back inside again.

"That's the last of them," Jack said as he stuffed two more papers into my bag. "Can you carry them?"

"Of course I can." I stood up and almost staggered under the weight. I'd never carried his bag when it was full and I was shocked by how much it weighed.

"Are you sure?"

"I'm sure," I groaned through clenched teeth.

"Now you know why the most popular routes are the ones that start close by. You can start unloading the bag right away instead of carting it halfway across town first." He started walking.

"Is Peter's route halfway across town?" I asked.

"No," he said, shaking his head.

"That's great!"

"It's actually *all* the way across town." Jack laughed. "But we'll deliver my route out of both bags, you on one side of the street and me on the other, and that way both bags will get lighter."

"Thanks."

Jack stopped in his tracks. "What's gotten into you?"

"What do you mean?"

"All this thanking me stuff. Stop it."

"Sorry," I apologized.

"And stop that, too! Quit being so mannerly."

"Sure . . . Shut up, Jack! Is that better?"

He smiled, and we walked another couple of blocks in friendly silence. "We're okay to talk here," Jack said after a while. "I didn't want to talk to Mr. Krum any more. He was awfully interested in the camp. He kept going on and on. He was making me nervous."

"Me too. He was asking me a lot of questions when we went inside to get the bag."

"He was? What sort of questions?"

"A lot of the same ones he was asking you. It was almost like he was checking to see if I was telling the truth."

"I don't know," Jack said. "He's got me wondering again."

"Come on, Jack, he isn't a spy. Remember what they said at the camp? If they'd thought he was a spy they'd have arrested him."

"But why else would he be so interested?"

"Because he's a newspaper guy. He wants to know because of what he does for a living."

"Maybe. Maybe not. All I know is that we especially can't talk to him about the camp."

"So if he asks any more questions we just say nothing, right?"

"Not nothing. We have to say something. The trick is to say nothing when we're saying something," he tried to explain.

"You lost me."

"We can't just pretend we have a zipper on our mouths and cover our ears with our hands when he asks questions. We have to answer him, but not tell him anything," Jack said.

"I'm still lost."

"Like when he asked about Corbett's Creek, I couldn't just pretend I didn't know it. I told him it was shallow in some places and deeper in others—like every other creek in the world."

"So if he asks me some more questions, what should I say?"

"Just nod your head and say something that really doesn't mean anything."

"I guess I can do that," I said. "Funny though."

"What's funny?" Jack asked.

"The day after we sign that oath saying we won't talk about what we saw, then somebody keeps asking us questions trying to get us to talk about it. It's almost like we were being tested."

Jack stopped walking and grabbed me by the arm. "Do you think?"

"Think what?" I asked.

"That Mr. Krum is actually working for them and they got him to ask us those questions."

"Who got him to ask us those questions . . . the Germans?"

"No, no, somebody working for the camp! He's part of them, and they asked him to question us to see if we were trustworthy."

I started to chuckle.

"Don't laugh!"

"I'm sorry, it's just that half a minute ago you thought he was a German agent, and now you think he's a spy for our side!"

"He could be," Jack argued. "They do have agents out here."

"You don't know that for sure."

"Yes I do. How else do you explain how they could take out the D.I.L. phones so Mom couldn't call, and how they made the bus break down? How do you explain that?"

I didn't have an answer, and I was beginning to wonder myself.

"So either Mr. Krum is nothing but a reporter, or he's a German spy, or he's an agent working with the camp," I said. "He could be anything."

"He could be. No matter what he is, though, we're not saying anything to him. Or anybody else. Matter of fact, I don't even want to talk to *you* about it any more. Let's just finish up the papers and go home for lunch."

# CHAPTER TWELVE

"I'LL GET IT!" I yelled as the phone rang out.

I threw the dishcloth onto the counter and ran for the phone. We'd just finished delivering the papers and were finishing up the breakfast dishes we'd left behind that morning.

"Hello?" I said as I picked it up.

"Hello. Is this Jack?" asked a man's voice. I didn't recognize it.

"No, this is George. I'll go and get—"

"That's all right. This is Bill."

"Bill?" My heart rose into my throat. "Bill from the . . . from the . . . place?"

"Did I make such a poor impression that you've almost forgotten me?"

"No, no, I just wasn't expecting you to call us."

"I told you we'd be in touch. Now go and get your brother so I can talk to both of you."

"Sure . . . yeah . . . right away!"

I dropped the phone and ran toward the kitchen. "Jack! Jack, come quick!" I yelled at the top of my lungs.

"What? What's wrong?" Jack looked annoyed.

"It's Bill," I said, my voice barely a whisper.

"Bill . . . Bill from the you-know-what?" Jack asked, lowering his voice.

I nodded my head.

"What does he want?"

"He said he wants to talk to us."

Jack rushed back and picked up the phone. "Hello . . . yep . . . um . . . yes." He nodded his head as he listened to words I couldn't hear.

"Now?" Jack asked. He seemed surprised.

That one word took my breath away. I had no idea what they were saying, but whatever it was it obviously couldn't wait.

"Okay, sure, we can do that. Bye."

Jack placed the receiver in its cradle.

"Go and make sure the front door is locked," he told me.

"Why?"

"Because Mom always likes us to lock the front door when we go out."

"Out where?" I asked anxiously.

Jack smiled. "I'm not entirely sure."

"But . . . but . . ."

"We're going out to the highway and we're going to be picked up."

"By who?" I demanded.

"Bill . . . or somebody he's sending to get us. Now go and check the door and let's get going."

"But what about the kitchen? We haven't finished cleaning up yet!"

"You can finish the kitchen if you want," Jack said, "and I'll go without you. I don't know what good a little crybaby like you could do anyway." He paused. "You coming or what?"

"I'm coming."

I ran and checked the front door. It was locked. I heard the side door slam and raced through the house to catch up with Jack. He was already outside and halfway up to the road. I chased after him, slowing to a walk when I finally came up beside him.

"Did he say anything more?" I asked.

"Sure."

"What else?"

"He said goodbye."

"Could you get serious? Did he say anything else about what we're doing?"

"Nothing except get to the highway and walk."

We cut through the vacant lot and took the path, coming out on the shoulder of the highway. A car whizzed by, followed by a swirl of dust. There were two more cars behind that one, and another coming in the opposite direction. None of them looked like the one that had dropped us off the other night.

"Which way do we walk?" I asked.

"He didn't say. Let's just walk toward the camp."

We started walking along the shoulder of the road, facing the oncoming traffic. A big truck rumbled toward us and I turned my head slightly to avoid the dust and gravel. We kept trudging along as car after car passed.

"Maybe we should have gone in the other direction."

"I don't know," Jack said.

"Are you sure he didn't say anything else?"

"I'm sure . . . almost as sure as I am that I wish I'd left you at—"

A car tooted its horn and we looked up. It was Chief Smith in his police cruiser, and as he passed he waved at us. Had Bill sent the Chief to get us? The car didn't even slow down as it continued along the highway.

"For a split second I thought he was the one we were meeting," Jack said, voicing my thoughts.

"That would have surprised me so much that it wouldn't even have surprised me," I said.

"What does that mean?" Jack asked.

"I don't think I understand anything that's been going on, and just as I think I do understand something I find out I'm wrong."

Jack started to laugh. "I thought it was only me who felt that way, and—"

My brother suddenly stopped mid sentence. Up ahead a dirty truck slowed down and pulled off to the side of the road.

"Is that them?" I asked.

In answer the back door of the truck popped open and Bill leaned out. "Hurry up, before somebody comes!" he yelled.

We both raced up and leaped into the truck. He slammed the door behind us, and before we could even settle down on the seats it started moving again. I grabbed onto the side of the seat to stop myself from being thrown backwards.

Besides Bill there was a driver and another man in the back. I'd never seen either of them before.

"We thought we'd gone the wrong way," Jack said.

"We had to wait until there was nobody else on the highway," Bill said. "That was the fourth time we'd passed you. We were heading in one direction when the chief of police honked his horn at the two of you. How does he know you boys?"

"He really doesn't," Jack said. "He was just talking to us one day."

"Do you know about him?" I asked.

"We know a lot of things," he said cryptically. "Just what did you mean specifically?"

"I mean that his family name is really Schmidt and he's of German descent?" I could tell that Jack hoped he was giving them information they didn't have. But he was out of luck.

"It's our business to know that kind of thing. And it pays to be observant." He turned around in his seat to look at us. "You must be wondering why we asked you to meet us."

"You said there was something you wanted to talk to us about," Jack said.

"Do you think you could do me a favour?"

"Sure, no problem," Jack said eagerly.

"Definitely," I agreed.

"I thought you boys were smarter than that."

Jack gave him a questioning look.

"It's wise to never agree to do anything you haven't heard yet. Want to hear about it?"

We both nodded our heads in agreement.

"I was hoping you could deliver a package for me. This package," he said, tapping his hand against a bag that sat at his side.

"Sure we can . . ." Jack stopped himself. "What is it?"

Bill started to laugh. "Now that's much better. It's a bomb."

"A bomb!" I gasped.

"And I want you to deliver it to the D.I.L. plant."

I felt a terrible rush of fear and confusion. "We can't do that!" I blurted out.

"We *won't* do that!" Jack growled.

What was going on? He was asking us to deliver a bomb to the plant where our mother worked. He wanted us to help him blow up the plant, and—

"Oh . . . I imagine I should have mentioned that it's a *fake* bomb? Here, have a look," he said as he opened up the bag. Inside were a few wires and a large chunk of clay.

"It's clay, isn't it? Like they used on the railroad bridge," Jack said.

"Yes, that's right, you did witness some of our men practicing the demolition of the trestle."

"I still don't understand why you use clay. Wouldn't it be better to use something that looks like sticks of dynamite?" Jack asked.

"It would if we used dynamite for our explosions. We use plastique."

"What's plastique?"

"It's a powerful new form of explosive. It resembles modelling clay. If a package of plastique as big as this hunk of clay were to explode it would create a crater in this road over thirty feet wide. And while pieces of this car would be flung in all directions for hundreds of feet, all that would remain of us would be a watery vapour rising into the air. They would not be able to determine how many people had been in this vehicle at the time of detonation."

"Wow," I said softly under my breath.

"I've never heard of it," Jack said.

"That's not surprising. It's very new. Our men are still getting used to it. Last winter some of them used plastique to blow up an ice dam that had formed on the creek. Used far too much of it and blew out windows for miles around."

"We heard about that!" I said.

"You did?" he asked, surprised. "Our records show you didn't move here until well after that incident."

"Mr. Krum told us," I explained.

"Mr. Krum knows a great deal," he said, and he didn't sound happy about it. "So, would you like to know why we're asking you to bring this fake bomb into the D.I.L. plant?"

"Yeah, why?" Jack asked.

"Part of our job is to find ways to destroy enemy targets. We need practice targets. At the same time, we have many sites that enemy agents might wish to destroy. By trying to 'blow up' these targets we not only practise our skills, we also learn how vulnerable our targets are to an actual enemy attack. We then tell them how to improve their security so they will be better protected."

"So it's like playing war," I said.

"It's not that simple," Jack argued.

"Actually it is. Our men are always playing war."

"You've done this before?"

"Oh my heavens, I think we've attacked the D.I.L. plant more than thirty times. It's one of our favourite targets because it's a prime location for enemy sabotage."

"And when you attack it, do you always get in?" Jack asked.

"Not always, but many times we have, and then they adjust their procedures to make it impossible, or at least much more difficult, to breach security in that manner."

"And you want us to break in?" I asked hesitantly.

"Certainly not," Bill said. "Breaking in could be quite dangerous. Their guards are well armed."

"But . . . but didn't you say you wanted us to deliver it?"

"Yes, but you're not going to break in. We want you two to walk right in the front gate. Let me explain."

I watched the panel truck travel down the road and get smaller and smaller until it disappeared. Up ahead was the hulking form of the D.I.L. plant. It was big and grey and topped by smokestacks billowing up clouds of dark smoke. All around the plant was a high metal fence, topped by strands of barbed wire. And all along the fence at regular intervals there were poles with lights on top. At night, when the lights were turned on, the grounds were as bright as day, and we could see the glow in the sky from our house, almost five miles away. I couldn't imagine how anybody could ever break in there without being seen.

We walked cautiously along the fence. Jack carried the paper bag tucked under his arm. At the driveway leading to the main gate there was a big guardhouse and a gate with a long striped arm blocking our way.

"I'll do the talking," Jack muttered to me as the guard stepped out of the guardhouse.

"Hello, boys, what can I do for you?"

"Our mom forgot her lunch this morning," Jack said, holding the bag up. "She called at break and asked us to bring it to her."

"Who's your mom?" he asked.

"Betty Braun."

"We came as fast as we could, but it's a long way to walk," I threw in. My brother shot me a murderous glance.

"How far did you come?" the guard asked.

"All the way from Whitby," Jack told him.

"My goodness, that was mighty nice of you boys to come all this way."

"Can we give it to her?" I asked innocently. "It's almost lunchtime and we have to walk all the way home again."

"Maybe I can make arrangements for you to get a ride on one of the trucks leaving here," he said. "They're not supposed to pick up people, but maybe I can convince one of the drivers to bend the rules a little."

"That would be great!" Jack said.

"I'll see what I can arrange while you boys go and deliver your mother her lunch. Do you know which section she works?"

"She works in J section."

"That's close. You go straight through the front door and take the corridor on your left. Look for the signs. You'll pass by sections N, M, L and—"

"That's okay, we know exactly where we're going," Jack said, cutting him off.

"Hurry right back, I think there's a truck getting ready to leave in thirty minutes."

"Thanks, we will," Jack said as we scurried around the big bar and walked toward the building.

Once we were out of sight Jack slugged me on the shoulder. "You were supposed to keep your mouth shut!"

"Yeah, but it worked, just like Bill said it would," I said under my breath, wincing a little.

"He didn't even look in the bag," Jack agreed.

"But what if he had?"

"Then we would have done what Bill said and told him to call the head of security and have him call Bill."

Jack held open the big door at the front. The foyer was empty. Off to the left was the corridor leading to where our mother was working. We turned to the right. There was a set of stairs and we started to climb, just as Bill had told us to do. We circled around and around and around, climbing to the top—four storeys up. There was a door there, and on the glass in large letters was the word "SECURITY."

Jack knocked loudly. The sound echoed down the stairwell. He knocked again.

"Hold on!" called out a voice.

I took a deep breath.

The door opened and a large man, dressed in a suit, stood there. He looked surprised to see us.

"Are you Mr. Granger?" Jack asked.

"Yes I am. And who are you two?"

"We've got a delivery for you," Jack said.

He went to take the bag from Jack, but Jack pulled it away. "First you have to read this." He handed the man a letter.

After he'd opened the envelope, he looked at us wide-eyed. He held the letter on an angle and I could see that written on it was one word in large print. It simply said "KABOOM!"

"I don't understand . . ." He looked up in confusion. "Is this some sort of a joke?"

"Bill said you'd understand," Jack said as he finally handed him the bag.

"Bill from the . . . Bill sent you?"

"Us and the bag."

He opened up the bag and slowly shook his head. "Clay."

"But it could have been something else," Jack pointed out.

"And you were able to sneak in here with this?"

"Not really sneak. We just walked in the front gate. We told the guard that we were bringing our mother her lunch because she forgot it."

"Your mother works here?" Mr. Granger asked.

I nodded.

"I didn't see this one coming . . . kids bringing in a fake bomb. I have to hand it to Bill. Nobody is more creative in figuring out how to destroy this place. The man is a genius! Thank goodness he trains agents for *our* side! Thanks to him, and the efforts of the other agents he's trained, I've been able to tighten up security in more than a dozen ways." He paused. "Do you think you two could do me a favour?"

"It depends," Jack said, turning and giving me a wink.

"Depends on what?" Mr. Granger asked.

"What the favour is," Jack explained.

"It's not difficult. I was just hoping you could deliver something to Bill."

"It depends on what it is," I said. It was my turn to wink at Jack.

Mr. Granger walked over to a filing cabinet and opened the bottom drawer. He pulled out a box. "These."

"What's in the box?" Jack asked.

I wondered if it was another fake bomb.

"Open it up and have a look," he said.

Jack removed the lid. It was a box of cigars.

"These are Bill's favourites, and he and I had a bet on whether or not he could infiltrate the plant this week. I lost. Again."

The phone on Mr. Granger's desk rang and he reached over and grabbed it.

"Hello? . . . I was wondering how long it would be until I heard from you."

Mr. Granger moved the phone away from his face and mouthed, "It's Bill."

"Yes, they are very nice young men, and I'll make sure that nobody here at the plant discovers the role they played. As far as the guard is concerned, they were only here to deliver a meal to their mother."

Mr. Granger listened as Bill spoke.

"Don't rub it in. I've already given the cigars to the boys to deliver to you."

Again he listened, nodded his head and then turned to us. "Bill will pick you up on the highway on the way back to Whitby."

"We already have a ride," I said.

"You do?"

"The guard is arranging for us to get a lift with a truck heading out of the plant," Jack explained.

Mr. Granger laughed out loud and then picked up the phone again. "Apparently your two agents have not only successfully blown up the plant, they've convinced one of our guards to break regulations and provide a get-away vehicle to escape the scene of the crime. These are definitely two of the best agents you've sent my way. I think they could easily break into your camp!"

Again Mr. Granger listened while Bill spoke. Then he laughed.

"I'll take that bet, double or nothing. Why don't you tell them?"

Mr. Granger passed the phone over to me.

"Hello, Bill, this is George."

"Hello, and congratulations to both you and your brother. You did an excellent job . . . first class."

"Thanks. We just did what you said."

"The best agents are often those who listen to their instructors the most closely. I was hoping that you could follow one more instruction. Could you bring me the cigars?"

"We already have a ride home, but maybe—"

"It doesn't have to be today. Anytime within the next few days would be fine. I'd like you and your brother to deliver them right here to the camp."

"Is there a front gate we should go to, like here at the plant?" I asked.

"There is a front gate, but if you go there you'll never get in."

"Why won't we?"

"Because nobody is allowed through the front gate without official clearance."

"But . . . but you want us to come."

"I want you to *try* to come. That's the subject of a little bet that Mr. Granger and I have just made. He believes that you and your brother could break into the camp. If you can successfully deliver these cigars to the main house then he will win. Are you interested in trying?"

"I need to ask, Jack," I said. I put the phone down to my side and turned to my brother. "Bill wants us to try to break into the camp. Do you want to do it?"

"Go on, give it a shot," Mr. Granger urged. "They try to

break into their own camp even more often than they try to break in here. It can only help security."

"When?" Jack asked.

"Anytime in the next few days," I said.

"Tell him we'll do it," Jack said, "if he has a soda waiting for both of us when we get there."

I smiled and picked up the phone. "Jack said that—"

"I heard him." Bill laughed. "Two sodas will be waiting at the officers' residence. Take care, and good luck!"

"Thanks," I said, and I returned the telephone to the cradle.

"Thank you for taking up the challenge, boys," Mr. Granger said. "Now all you need is an advantage."

"What do you mean?" Jack asked.

"Surprise is the advantage you need. He's expecting you in the next few days. How about if you try to sneak into the camp in the next few minutes? I'm proposing that we leave, climb into my car, and I can have you at the edge of the camp within fifteen minutes. What do you think?"

"I think that might work," Jack said. "But could you drive us to our house first? We have to pick up a couple of inner tubes."

# CHAPTER THIRTEEN

THE WATER FELT AWFULLY good. I would have liked to have just soaked and swum, but there was no time. We had less than three hours before Mom got home. I sat on my inner tube, paddling frantically with both hands. Jack floated behind his, kicking with his feet. On top of his tube, held in place with twine, was a canvas sack, oiled to make it waterproof, that contained the box of cigars. We hoped it could withstand a dunking without water seeping through and destroying the contents.

I wasn't so sure that three hours would give us long enough to get in and back before Mom arrived home from work, but Jack said that was plenty of time. Either we'd be caught and it would be over, or we'd get in quickly and perhaps somebody would drive us home. And even if we were an hour or so late we could just tell Mom we were out playing and lost track of time.

"I'm not so sure this will work," I told him. "Won't they be expecting us to come in this way because we did it before?"

"First off we have the element of surprise. Second, we're going in a *different* way."

"How do you figure that?"

"We'll keep floating down the creek until we hit the lake."

"What good will that do? Won't they be able to see us bobbing up and down on the water?"

"Don't you remember anything that Mr. Granger told us in the car?"

"Some things."

Jack shook his head. He said there's a marsh at the end of the creek and then high cliffs along part of the lake. First we'll be hidden by the reeds and then by the cliffs."

"But if there are cliffs, how do we get up to the buildings?"

"We climb."

"Up the cliffs?"

"We'll just look for the right spot. It won't be that hard . . . at least I don't think it will. Then again, maybe we should try to come in through the marsh. We'll just sort of play it by ear."

That wasn't the reassurance I was looking for. I'd hoped he had some sort of master plan in mind.

The creek cut through a grove of trees, and the branches on both sides reached above the water and formed a canopy over our heads. I stopped paddling and looked up. Little bits of blue and stripes of sunshine broke through. I liked it there. I felt protected and secret, as if it was a little hiding spot instead of out in the open. It would have been so nice to have just stayed there.

"Hurry up!" Jack yelled back over his shoulder.

I dug in my hands and started paddling again.

We rounded a bend in the creek. Up ahead I could see the big willow, and then the trestle beyond that. I paddled harder with my left hand to push the tube out more into the centre of the stream. I wanted to go through the middle span of the trestle again.

I looked up at the bridge. There was nothing there—nobody. Then I scanned the bank of the creek as far along as I could see. Again, nothing that I could see, but there were hundreds of places somebody could have been sitting, watching us. We were completely exposed. It would have been different if we'd come at night . . . but there was no way I was ever coming here at night, so that didn't matter.

I tilted my head back as I neared the trestle. It looked higher and higher the closer I got. Finally I bent my head right back and watched the bridge float by above my head, until I popped out the other side. First Jack and then I passed by the spot where we'd brought the tubes in before. Everything from there on was new.

The creek cut sharply to the left and then almost immediately to the right. I anxiously scanned the banks of the creek, first one side and then the other. I couldn't see anybody.

I looked up ahead. Jack was almost out of sight. I began to paddle furiously to try to close the gap. Despite my efforts it seemed as if Jack was pulling away, picking up speed. I dug in deeper to try to get closer. He was moving fast . . . we were both moving fast. The banks of the creek seemed to be closing in and the current was picking up speed. Suddenly the stream dipped down and I felt myself being thrown forward. I grabbed on tight . . . then it dipped again, but this time I was ready. Stretching ahead were a series of dips, and rocks, and white water. I had a rush of fear that matched the rush of the water around me. I wanted to try to get to the side of the creek, get out of the flow, but I couldn't let Jack get away. He was at the very end of a long straight section, being towed behind his tube. As long as I could keep him in sight I'd be—he disappeared from view! Had the creek cut to the side? Or . . . had he? Oh my God!

"Aaaahhhh!" I screamed as I shot off into space and then plunged down, head first, still clinging to the tube with one hand. I dropped beneath the water and my grip on the tube pulled me back to the surface. I looked back. I'd just come over a waterfall! It had to be more than six feet high!

I turned back around. Jack was standing in shallow water off to the side. He was holding his punctured inner tube—or what was left of it—in one hand.

"Are you okay?" I yelled.

"Be quiet!" he hissed.

I swam over to him, pulling my tube behind me. Jack was now sitting on the shore. The bottom rose up quickly, making it shallow enough for me to put my feet down. As I waded in, Jack untied the oiled sack from the remains of the tube. He opened up the flap and turned the bag upside down. Water poured out.

"I'd be afraid to look inside," I said.

"I'm not going to," Jack muttered. "We promised we'd deliver them. We didn't promise what shape they'd be in when they got there."

"What are we going to do now?" I asked.

"We still go down the creek."

"Are you going to share my tube?"

"Not much choice."

Jack slipped the box of cigars back into the oiled bag—not that it really mattered much now. He then took the twine and tied it around my tube.

"You climb back in," he said. "And I'll hang on to the back."

Jack steadied the tube while I climbed onto it. He pushed us back into the middle and we started to move. There didn't seem to be much current. The waterfall drained into a large pool, and the creek was much wider after that.

"Keep your eyes open," Jack said. "One waterfall was one more than I wanted to go over."

I hadn't even thought about that. Quickly the bushes and trees on the banks became sparse and then vanished completely. In their place bullrushes and marsh grass rose up on both sides of us. Jack continued to kick, pushing us forward slowly. Up ahead there were a number of channels cutting through the growth.

"Which way do we go?" I asked.

"We'll go to the left. That's the closest to the camp."

We drifted down the channel, closed in on all sides. We were moving even more slowly now.

"Is there any current at all?" I asked.

"Not much. Climb off and help me kick."

Reluctantly I slid off and into the water. It didn't look particularly clean, but it certainly felt warm. I joined Jack and started to kick my feet. Slowly we moved forward.

"I can touch," Jack said. He stood up and the water was below his waist.

I set my feet down. It was soggy and I sank slightly into the muddy bottom. Good thing I was wearing my shoes. Gradually the reeds gave way as the water got shallower and shallower. Finally Jack picked up the tube and carried it under his arm. We climbed up a sandy slope and out of the water. I slumped to the ground and Jack plopped down beside me. Up ahead there were a few trees and some shrubs that blocked our view. They also blocked anybody's view of us.

"We'll leave the tube right here and walk in," Jack said.

What I really wanted to do was just stay there on the sand, at least for a while. I wanted to dry out and rest, but I knew we didn't have time to stop. I trailed behind Jack as he moved into the trees. At least there was more cover there.

"I'm trying to picture where the buildings are from here," Jack said. "They're more on the other side of the property, but the stream cut in sharper than I thought it was going to."

"I don't think the trees go on much farther," I said.

Slowly we crept to the edge of the cover. Hiding behind a bush we looked out. There was a large, empty, open field stretching out in front of us. In the distance, directly across, were the buildings. We weren't as far away as we'd thought!

"We're practically there," Jack said.

"*Practically* and *there* are two different things. What now?" I asked.

"We can follow the trees and try to go around," Jack suggested.

I looked first in one direction and then the others. Off to one side, way in the distance, trees ringed the meadow.

"Can we do that and still get home in time?" I asked.

Jack shook his head. "Probably not. Do you see anybody?"

"Nobody . . . why?"

"I was just thinking."

"Not about making a run for it, I hope."

"It wouldn't take us more than sixty seconds if we ran flat out, twice as long if we just sort of trotted. Let's try it."

"Jack, we really shouldn't do—"

Before I could finish Jack had jumped up and started to jog across the field. I had no choice. I burst out of the bushes after him. I swivelled my head from side to side. There was nobody in sight. Maybe we could make it. I came alongside Jack. The buildings were getting closer and closer. I started to pump my legs faster, trying to move more quickly, and pulled slightly ahead of my brother.

"Shoot!" Jack said as he grabbed my arm and forcibly pulled me to a stop.

"What's wrong?" I sputtered, before I saw the answer in the distance. A jeep had popped out from a gap between the trees and was moving along the edge of the field.

"We lose," Jack said. "There's no way they can miss seeing us."

"I guess you're . . . hold on . . . maybe they *should* see us," I said. "Hey!" I yelled, waving my hands in the air. "Over here!"

Jack grabbed me by the arm and spun me around. "What are you doing?"

I shook off his hand. "Making sure they see us. Hey, over here!"

The men in the jeep had now altered their course and were coming right for us.

"We still had a chance," Jack said sullenly as the jeep closed in. "We could have made a break for it, or—"

"There was no way they would have missed us. Just shut up and let *me* do the talking this time."

"Don't you tell *me* to shut up!" he snapped. "And what do you mean let *you* do the talking?"

"Shut up," I repeated. "I have a plan."

My brother looked as if he was going to take a swing at me, but he buttoned his lip.

The jeep rumbled toward us. There were two soldiers, a driver and another man in the passenger seat.

"Now remember . . . keep your trap shut," I hissed at him as the jeep pulled to a stop beside us.

"Hi guys!" I called out. I recognized both of them from the different times we'd been caught. "We're looking for Bill, have you seen him?"

"Not for a while," one of them answered.

"The Lieutenant-Colonel asked us to deliver this to Bill," I said, taking the box from my brother's hand. "We were told it was important and that he'd either be at the beach or over by the farmhouse."

"What's in the package?" the other soldier asked.

I shrugged. "We're just delivery boys. They don't tell us what we're delivering. He just said it was important. Do you think you could give us a lift to the farmhouse?"

"We're going that way anyway, jump in," the driver offered.

"Smooth," Jack whispered to me as we circled around to the back and climbed in.

The jeep started up and tightly turned to head toward the buildings. The passenger turned around in his seat.

"I didn't expect to see you boys here again." He yelled so his voice could be heard over the engine and the rushing air.

"They have us doing lots of different things," Jack yelled back. "You'd be surprised what we're up to!"

The jeep bumped across the field until it hit a gravel road at the edge. The tires bit into the gravel as we sped along, but the driver slowed down as we passed by the first building. I saw the farmhouse right up ahead.

"You're in luck, boys, there's Bill!" the driver called out.

I stood slightly up and peered between the two men. There was Bill standing with the Lieutenant-Colonel and another man.

The jeep skidded to a stop right in front of them.

"Thanks for the ride!" I said to the men as I leaped over the side of the jeep.

"No problem," one of them called back.

I looked up at Bill. He looked as if he'd seen a ghost.

"Here are your cigars," I said as I handed him the box. "They might be a little wet."

"Maybe you can give them back to Mr. Granger to pay off your end of the bet," Jack suggested.

Bill stood there, silent, his mouth open. The Lieutenant-Colonel looked just as shocked.

"Perhaps somebody would be so good as to explain this to me," the man beside them said. "Inside. Now. In private."

# CHAPTER FOURTEEN

"PLEASE, GENTLEMEN, WOULD YOU take a seat?" the man said as we entered the Lieutenant-Colonel's office.

He walked over and sat down on a chair right beside the ones we'd taken. The Lieutenant-Colonel stood behind his desk, and Bill waited off to the side.

"You gentlemen should sit as well," he said, and they each took a seat. I didn't know who this man was, but he was clearly older than the other two, and he certainly acted as though he was in charge.

"It's past tea time, but would either of you care for a cup?" he asked.

"No, thank you," I said.

"We were hoping for a soda," Jack added. "Wasn't that part of the bet?"

"You'd mentioned a bet outside," the man said. "I'm interested in pursuing that line of questioning, but first I must ask your forgiveness for my lack of manners." He reached out, offering his hand.

Jack reached out his hand to shake. "I'm Jack, and this is my brother, George."

He reached out and shook my hand next.

"I'm Bill," he said.

"There are two Bills?"

"It *is* a common name. Many people refer to me as 'Little Bill,' if that helps."

He certainly wasn't nearly as tall or wide as our Bill. He was wearing a suit and tie and he looked very gentle, almost friendly. His voice was soft and reassuring. He reminded me of a teacher or a minister. He had sort of a pointy nose, but what really stood out were his eyes—they were sharp and bright and penetrating.

"Now tell me about this bet," he said.

"It's nothing really," Bill said. "It involves Mr. Granger from over at the D.I.L. plant. He and I have this running—"

"Excuse me." Little Bill cut him off, his voice rising slightly. "I was asking the boys. Besides, shouldn't you be going and getting them their sodas?"

"Well, I was just trying . . . " He stopped mid sentence as Little Bill's eyes flashed. Suddenly he didn't seem like a teacher or minister. He looked angry and intense and I felt frightened, even though he wasn't looking at me.

"I'll go right now, sir," Bill said, and then he spun on his heels briskly and left the room.

Bill had called him "sir," so whoever he was he outranked him, even though he wasn't wearing a uniform.

"Now what does this bet have to do with the D.I.L. plant?" Once again his voice was quiet and calm and his eyes were friendly.

"Bill asked us to deliver a fake bomb to the plant."

"Interesting. And when was this request made?"

"Today. We did it today," Jack said.

"And can I assume you were successful?"

"It was easy!" I told him. "We just walked in the front gate and asked if we could deliver a lunch to our mother."

"She works there," Jack added.

"And then Mr. Granger and Bill were talking, and they agreed to double the bet if we could break in here and deliver these to Bill," I said, offering him the box, which I was still holding.

He took it from my hands and carefully removed the lid.

"Soggy cigars?"

"They didn't start out soggy. My inner tube ripped open when we came over the waterfall," Jack explained.

"A waterfall?"

"We didn't even know it was there until we went over it!" I exclaimed.

"I certainly hope it wasn't too big a waterfall," he said, kindly.

"Bigger than I would have liked," I said, and he chuckled softly in response.

"And how exactly did you come to navigate over a waterfall of any size?"

"We were trying to sneak into the camp from Corbett's Creek. That's how we've done it before," Jack explained.

Little Bill now turned to the Lieutenant-Colonel. "They've come onto the base before?"

"Three times," he answered hesitantly. "But we did manage to capture them twice."

"I suppose I should be impressed by that percentage," Little Bill said, but he didn't sound impressed.

"That's partly where I got the idea for tricking those two men in the jeep," I explained. "I recognized them from before, and I knew that they knew us."

"So we just called them over," Jack continued. He turned to me. "My brother just called them over."

"It was sort of like how we brought the bag of clay into the plant. We just acted like we belonged and the guards thought we did."

Little Bill didn't say anything. He was holding one of the cigars in his hands and rolling it back and forth, deep in thought.

"These would certainly provide a very clever way to transport plastique," he said to the Lieutenant-Colonel. "I wonder how much explosive could be placed in the middle of a cigar, hidden by tobacco."

"Probably enough to blow up a car," Jack offered.

He turned back to us. "I suppose I shouldn't be too surprised that you two know about plastique. They haven't actually allowed you to blow anything up, have they?"

"No," I said. "Do you think we could?"

He smiled. "I don't think that would be a wise option."

"We have seen how it's supposed to work, though," Jack went on.

Again Little Bill turned to the Lieutenant-Colonel.

"On one of their trips onto the grounds they witnessed a mock attempt by four of our agents to blow up a train while it was on a trestle," the Lieutenant-Colonel explained.

The door opened and Bill walked in carrying a tray. On it sat a teapot, some cups, milk and sugar, and two bottles of orange pop. He set it down on the table beside Little Bill.

"Let me pour," Little Bill said.

He picked up the pot and steam rose as he carefully poured tea into three china cups.

"Sugar and milk?" he asked the Lieutenant-Colonel.

"One lump and a dash of milk, please."

He took the tongs and placed a single lump of sugar in the cup and then added a little milk.

"And what would you like?" he asked Bill.

"Just milk, please."

He poured milk and then handed the cup and saucer to Bill.

"And, boys, why don't you have your sodas," he said, as he passed the bottles over to us.

I immediately took a sip. It tasted cold and sweet and refreshing. What with the shortage of sugar, it was pretty rare for us to actually have a soda.

Little Bill proceeded to pour himself a cup of tea. The only sound in the room was the Lieutenant-Colonel's spoon clinking against his china cup.

"So," Little Bill began, "if I am to understand correctly, in the space of a few short hours these two young men have managed to infiltrate both a secure manufacturing plant and this highly restricted training school."

Bill and the Lieutenant-Colonel nodded their heads in agreement.

"We just did what Bill told us," I explained. "He sort of trained us."

"Indeed," Little Bill said. "He trained you very well. Bill, if you would now explain things further I would appreciate it."

Bill took a quick sip from his tea and set the cup down in the saucer.

"I was thinking that our enemy seems to know little in the way of moral boundaries in warfare, so I suspected that they would put no limits on their conduct of espionage."

"What does that mean?" I said it before I realized that I shouldn't be saying anything. "I'm sorry."

"Don't be, George," Little Bill said. "It means that the Nazis don't ever fight in a fair or honourable manner. They will do whatever it takes to win, regardless of what they need to do to reach that goal."

"Exactly," Bill said. "And I reasoned that they wouldn't be above using children, or pregnant women or old people, to their advantage, to deliver bombs and such. I needed some way to test this theory, so I asked the boys to help."

"And indeed they did." Little Bill paused and took a long sip of his tea. "You boys of course realize that nothing of what has happened can be discussed with anybody."

"We signed the oath," Jack said.

"But we wouldn't have told anybody anyway," I added.

"When did they sign the secrecy oath?" Little Bill asked.

"After they were found on the grounds the second time

and we became aware of just how much they had observed," the Lieutenant-Colonel explained.

"And as a result of interviewing the boys we've made significant changes to the security here at the camp," Bill added anxiously.

"Have you?" Little Bill asked. "And I suppose some other changes may still be in order, wouldn't you think?"

Bill looked down at his cup. I felt so bad about getting him in trouble.

"I believe an order should be given to all members of the camp concerning any and all visitors previously known. I'll leave that to your expertise to institute. Please have a word with the gentlemen who drove the boys into the compound." He paused and took another sip of tea. "Remember, a mistake is only a mistake if you fail to learn from it."

"Yes, sir," Bill said. "I'll go right now and make those—"

"Please, that can wait until we've finished our visit with Jack and George. So, gentlemen, your mother works at the munitions plant. And your father?"

"Would you like their files?" the Lieutenant-Colonel asked.

"Oh, no, certainly not. This is tea, not an interrogation," he answered. "So where is your father?"

"He's in the army," I said.

"In Africa serving with the St. Patrick's Regiment," Jack added.

"I know that regiment. It is composed entirely of men who volunteered to fight for King and country. You must be very proud of your father."

"We are," Jack said.

"And if he were to know what you have done here he would be proud of you both."

"He would?" I was startled to realize that Jack and I had asked the question in unison.

"Most certainly. Are you aware that you have helped your father?"

Jack gave me a confused look—one that I was sure was mirrored on my face.

"You have assisted the men who are training and being trained here. That help will be of benefit to our side in a most terrible form of war. Do you know anybody who has been through a war?"

"Our Uncle Jack was in the First World War," my brother said. "I'm named after him."

"And there's Mr. Krum, too," I added. "He was a hero."

Bill and the Lieutenant-Colonel looked up from their tea and stared at me. Had I said something wrong?

"Can I refill your cups?" Little Bill asked as he lifted the teapot.

Both men held out their cups and he poured more tea. He then added milk to both cups and another cube of sugar to one.

"I wasn't aware you two knew Mr. Krum," Little Bill said.

"I have a paper route," Jack answered.

"And I help out, but Mr. Krum said I could have a route of my own soon . . . maybe."

"I'm sure you'd do an excellent job, George. And Mr. Krum has spoken to you boys about the last war, has he?"

"Not much about the war," Jack said.

"That doesn't surprise me. Does your Uncle Jack ever tell you tales of the war?"

"Never. He doesn't talk about it at all."

"It was . . . a terrible war. I had hoped that we had learned from it, but I was sadly mistaken."

"Were you in that war?" I asked.

He nodded his head ever so slightly.

"Were you in the army?"

"I started in the army. But a gas attack ended my days as a soldier. I was too sick to ever return to the trenches."

"That's too bad," I said.

"I thought so too. So I learned to fly above the trenches instead. I became a pilot."

"You flew one of those old-fashioned airplanes?"

He nodded his head and smiled. I guess I shouldn't have called them that, but he didn't seem to mind.

"They certainly seem that way, looking back, but at the time we thought of them as the finest things imaginable."

"And Little Bill was among the best," the Lieutenant-Colonel hastened to tell us. "He was an ace and was highly decorated."

"I don't think we should talk of that," Little Bill said. "Far too embarrassing."

"Do you still have your medals?" I asked.

Little Bill didn't answer right away, but he took a long sip from his cup. "I have them . . . I think they're in an old tobacco tin in my hall closet."

"Not in a fancy case?" Jack asked.

"That's how Mr. Krum keeps his," I added.

"Mr. Krum has shown you his medals?"

"Yeah, he has a bunch," I told them.

"Indeed. He was highly decorated."

"You've seen them too?" I asked.

Bill and the Lieutenant-Colonel burst into laughter and I felt embarrassed for asking.

"I can understand why you would think that," Little Bill said, defending me. "I am familiar with Mr. Krum by other means."

"Like the file you have on him?" Jack guessed.

"What makes you think we have a file on him?"

"Because he tried to get in here once," I said. "Like us."

"He said he was following a truck filled with lumber because he wanted to see what was being built here."

"That, and other reasons," Little Bill said, taking another sip of his tea.

"You mean because he's the editor of the paper?" I asked.

"That is significant."

"My brother thought he was a spy."

Jack shot me a dirty look. I knew I'd pay for opening my mouth once we got home.

"A spy?" Little Bill asked. "Why would you think that?"

"Well . . . he was asking about the camp," Jack explained.

"And when he asked what did you say?"

"Nothing."

"Mostly we just listened. He already knew a lot," Jack added. "He was the one who told us that it was a special army base."

"And Jack didn't believe him at first when he said this was an army base."

"You didn't?" Little Bill asked.

Jack shook his head slowly and looked even more embarrassed.

"What did you think was going on here?"

"I sort of thought it was like, maybe, it was a German spy base," he said quietly.

"That's why we kept sneaking into the place. We were looking for spies. But of course we know better now. We know Mr. Krum's not a spy. He's just asking questions because he's a newspaperman. He's just being nosy, even though he knows he can't print what he finds."

Little Bill took another sip of his tea. A long, slow sip. His expression remained calm, but his eyes seemed to get dark and stormy.

"Do you boys think there might be spies about here?"

I shrugged. "I don't know . . . maybe, I guess."

"Perhaps I've been in this line of work too long, but I believe there are agents of the enemy at work throughout this country."

"Chief Smith could be a spy," I blurted out.

"Chief Smith?" Little Bill asked.

"He's the head of the local police force," Bill explained.

"But really his name isn't even Smith," I said. "It's Schmidt, and that's a German name."

"Indeed," Little Bill said. "It's as German as, say . . . Braun."

Suddenly I was the one who felt embarrassed.

"Now if you boys will excuse us I must talk to the Lieutenant-Colonel."

I put down my empty soda bottle and stood up along with Jack. Little Bill rose to his feet as well.

"It has been a pleasure to meet two such fine young men." He reached out and shook our hands. "Bill, would you be so kind as to arrange to bring them home?"

"Thanks. And goodbye," Jack said, and then Bill ushered us from the room, closing the door behind him and leaving the two men alone in the Lieutenant-Colonel's office.

"I suppose the first thing I should do after dropping you two at home is call Mr. Granger and inform him that I now owe him *two* boxes of cigars," Bill said.

"Sorry about that," Jack offered.

"And about getting you in trouble," I added.

"Nothing to be sorry about. I've been told to fix things, and nothing more will be made of it. Little Bill is like that."

"Is he in charge of the camp?" I asked.

"This camp? He's in charge of a whole lot more than this camp." Bill laughed. "I can't really say anything else, but I want you two boys to remember this meeting. One day, probably long after the war is won, you'll learn just who that was."

"He must be important," I said.

"More than I can say. Come on, let's get you two home before your mother gets back from work."

# CHAPTER FIFTEEN

"IF YOU'D LEARN TO count we wouldn't have this problem," Jack snorted.

"I can count! I guess I just . . . sort of . . . counted wrong."

Peter Cook was sick again and I was doing his route. Unfortunately, when I'd got to the end of my newspapers I still had five more houses left to deliver to. Somehow I hadn't taken enough papers.

"Walking across town once to deliver the papers was bad enough, but having to go back a second time to pick up extras," Jack grumbled, shaking his head, "that's even worse."

"You don't have to come with me."

"Yeah, right, and if Mom finds out I didn't, then you know whose head it'll be."

We walked along in silence for a few houses.

"Do you think we'll see him again?" I asked.

"See who?"

"Little Bill."

"Probably not. But I didn't think we'd ever see anybody from the base again, and then Bill called us. So who knows?"

"Who do you think he was?"

"Some sort of general or something. Do spies have a general?" he wondered.

"Beats me, but they do have a boss. Everybody has a boss . . . don't they?"

"I guess so, and we'd better get those papers and get them delivered before somebody calls our boss and complains."

We doubled our pace, cutting through an alley that led to the back of the newspaper offices, where the loading dock was located.

"I just hope there are still five papers left," Jack said.

"Why wouldn't there be?"

"The papers all get sent out by truck to be delivered to stores after the paper boys take what they need."

"There's *got* to be five papers left over."

"Let's hope."

What I could see from this distance was that the two newspaper trucks were gone from the back. That wasn't a good sign. They'd left with their loads of papers.

"Let's hurry," I said.

"I'll tell you something, George. Either there's enough papers still at the office or you're going to have to hurry a lot more."

"What do you mean?"

"You're going to have to run and catch the trucks!"

I jumped up onto the loading dock. It wasn't just the

trucks that were gone, the whole place was deserted. Except for some office staff—I could hear a phone ringing in the inner office and the sounds of typing.

Jack went over to the sorting table. "There are only three papers here," he said. He walked over and dropped them in my bag. I looked over by the big printing press. There were scraps, pages that hadn't printed right, but nothing near a complete paper.

"Maybe we have to ask inside," I suggested.

"No choice."

We walked past the presses and into the office. There were two people seated at desks: Mrs. Perkins, who answered the telephones, and Mr. Jennings, who was one of the reporters. He was a nice, older man. She was a not-so-nice, old woman. She continually looked like she'd just bitten down on something sour. I would have liked to ask Mr. Jennings about the papers, but he was on the phone. Mrs. Perkins was free.

I stopped in front of her desk. "Hi."

She looked up but didn't answer.

"I was short some papers for the route. Do you know where we could get two more?"

"The store."

"What store?" I asked.

"Any store across the whole county. They've all gone out. Why didn't you take the papers you needed?"

Jack came to my defence, as usual. "He's not a regular paper boy, he was just doing Mr. Krum a favour because Peter Cook is sick again!"

"Then maybe you should ask Mr. Krum," she suggested. "He's in his office."

I hesitated. I didn't want to talk to Mr. Krum. He'd been out by the loading dock when we'd been sorting our papers, and he'd really wanted to talk. We'd worked as quickly as possible so we wouldn't be left alone with him. That was probably the reason I'd counted wrong in the first place, because we'd been so anxious to leave.

"I assume you know where his office is located?" Mrs. Perkins snapped.

"Thanks," I said.

Jack and I walked slowly toward his closed door. I lifted my hand and knocked.

"Wait!" called out Mr. Krum.

We stood by the door, unable to enter, but unable to leave either. I had to fight the urge to turn around and run. The door opened, and Mr. Krum was standing there. His expression changed from angry to surprised to welcoming in the space of just a second.

"Jack, George! What can I do for you two?"

"I sort of miscounted papers and I need a few more," I explained.

"The trucks have already left. How many are you short?"

"Two."

"That is not a problem. I believe there should be two or three left at the sorting table."

"We already got three from there," Jack pointed out. "We're still two short."

"There can be only one answer then," Mr. Krum said. "Come with me."

"Where?"

"I'll drive you to the store and we'll pick up two papers."

"That's okay. We can walk," Jack told him.

"I'm sure you could, but you would have to purchase the papers, whereas I can simply take them. Come."

Jack and I hesitated, but I didn't see any choice. How could we explain not going with him? So what if he asked a few questions? We didn't have to say anything. We trailed Mr. Krum out of his office.

"Mrs. Perkins, I am going out," Mr. Krum announced. "I will not be returning today, so I leave things in your reliable hands."

She nodded her head but didn't say a word.

Mr. Krum opened the front door and the bell attached to the frame pinged loudly, making me jump. His car was parked just outside the office. It was a big, black sedan.

The editor climbed into his car, then reached over and unlocked the passenger door, pushing it open. Jack gave me a little shove so I had to climb in first. He sat down beside me and closed the door as Mr. Krum started the engine.

"This is most fortunate that you two came back. I was hoping to talk to you," Mr. Krum began.

"What did you want to talk about?" Jack asked him.

"Many things."

"About me getting my own route?" I hoped.

"Perhaps. You know it is important for me to trust the

people that work for me. Trust is very important, don't you think?"

"I'm sorry about the papers . . . I won't forget to count again," I apologized.

"Coming back to get the papers was a sign that you are responsible. I'm referring more to trusting somebody to be honest."

I bit the side of my cheek.

"George, do you always do that when you are nervous?" Mr. Krum asked.

"Do what?"

"Bite your cheek."

"Not always," I said, stopping myself.

"There is nothing to be nervous about, George. I assure you, I am not angry at you for needing my assistance to get more papers."

"Mr. Krum, we just passed the store," Jack pointed out.

"We're not going to that store. It would not have papers yet. It is one of the last deliveries on the driver's route. So, wouldn't you agree that trust and honesty are things that an employer should expect from those he employs?"

"Yeah, definitely," Jack answered.

"We're honest, honest," I said.

"I believe that of you both. Now, I was wondering if you would be good enough to answer a few questions."

"Sure," Jack said.

"Of course."

"I was wondering how you know Mr. Granger."

I swallowed hard but didn't answer. Jack remained silent as well.

"I saw him drive you boys home yesterday from the D.I.L. plant."

"Oh, is that his name?" Jack asked. "He works at the plant."

"He's the head of security at the plant," Mr. Krum said.

"We didn't know that," Jack said. "We had to drop off our mother's lunch."

"She forgot it and asked us to bring it," I added.

"And he just offered to drive us home afterward."

"That was very kind of him," Mr. Krum observed.

"He was just driving our way is all," Jack continued. "I'm not sure where he was going to."

"Really? It appeared he was going to Corbett's Creek. At least, that's where he dropped you two off."

I felt the colour drain from my face.

"You were following us?" Jack asked.

"It is as I said, newspapermen are always curious."

"I meant that I didn't know where he went after he dropped us off." Jack was thinking fast. "We wanted to go for a swim and we needed to get our suits and inner tubes."

"A long swim. You did not reappear for over two hours."

"You waited for us?"

"For over two hours. Did you go onto the Sinclair farm?"

"No, of course not," Jack lied.

"We haven't been back to the camp," I added.

"The camp . . . strange that you should call it that."

"That's what *you* call it," Jack said.

"No. Never. I refer to it as the Sinclair property or the farm or even Glenrath, but never the camp."

"But I must have heard it from you."

"No. The only people who refer to it as the camp are the spies who are being trained there."

"Spies . . . what do you mean spies?" Jack asked innocently.

Mr. Krum turned and looked at us. His expression left little doubt that he thought—he knew—that Jack was lying.

"Have you . . . have you . . . been talking to some of the people there?" I asked him.

"No, but apparently you two have."

"No, we haven't."

"Please do not lie to me, Jack." His voice was very calm and his eyes were now trained on the road again.

"Well, if you haven't been talking to any of them, how do you even know what they call the place?" Jack asked.

"I've been listening to their radio messages."

"You have? But . . . how . . . and why?" I asked.

Mr. Krum answered by speeding the car up. We had left the last street behind and turned onto the highway.

"We have to get home," Jack told him, firmly.

"I am afraid that will not be possible."

"But our mother is expecting us. You can't just take us!" he exclaimed.

"I am afraid it is necessary. I believe you have found a way into that camp, and I need to know how."

"We're not saying anything. Stop the car!" Jack yelled.

Mr. Krum took his right hand off the steering wheel. He

slipped it into the inside pocket of his jacket and removed a pistol.

"You will remain quiet and calm," he said as he aimed it in our direction. "I want you both to slip off the seat and onto the floor of the car."

I looked over at Jack and then at the gun. Reluctantly we slid down onto the floor.

# CHAPTER SIXTEEN

I EDGED OVER ON the floor toward Jack, trying to gain a few more inches of separation from Mr. Krum. I just wished I hadn't been the first in, because then I would have had Jack between me and our captor . . . as if that would have protected me. We drove along in silence. The only noises were the droning of the engine and the rush of vehicles whizzing past us in the other direction. I could just catch a glimpse of the roofs as they raced past. I tried not to, but I couldn't help looking over at Mr. Krum. The pistol remained firmly in Mr. Krum's hand . . . his shaking hand. Why was *he* shaking? He was the one with the gun . . . A *gun*. Now it was *my* turn to start shaking.

The car started to slow down. Mr. Krum turned the wheel and I could tell from the sound of the tires against the ground that we'd turned onto an unpaved road. We travelled a few car lengths and then he brought it to a stop. Was this where we were going?

"There is a chain across the lane," Mr. Krum said, quietly and calmly. "Jack, you are to get out and unlock it so that we may proceed. The key is under the large rock behind the post."

Jack didn't move.

"Do as you are told," he said, pointing the pistol at my brother.

Jack pushed himself up and onto the seat and then opened the door and started to step out.

"Attempting to run would not be wise . . . I would not like to have to shoot you, and your brother."

My whole body tingled with fear.

Jack nodded his head and climbed out of the car.

"You may sit on the seat now," Mr. Krum told me.

"What?"

"There is no need for you to be on the floor . . . take the seat."

I climbed up and watched Jack. He had pushed the rock aside and was reaching down to get the key. Part of me wanted him to just bolt away, while the rest of me was terrified. Mr. Krum would shoot at him . . . maybe he wouldn't be able to escape. And me . . . I'd be as good as dead.

I moved slightly over again, away from Mr. Krum. Just behind us I heard the rush of air as another car passed. I looked over my shoulder. It was already gone. We were no more then a few dozen yards away from the highway. Maybe somebody would see us, or maybe I could get to the road and run for help. The door was beside me, open, ever so close. Maybe I could just—

"Do not even let that thought into your mind, George," Mr. Krum said.

I froze in place.

Jack fumbled with the lock and then it popped open and he released the chain. It fell to the ground with a thump. He came back to the car and climbed back in, landing partly on top of me. I wasn't going to move over. Awkwardly, Jack closed the car door.

Mr. Krum set the car back in motion and we moved down the long farm lane. The way was rough, potholed and rutted. On both sides there was thick brush and trees. We kept going until we came up to a small farmhouse. The little front porch was sagging on one side, and one of the panes of glass in the front window had been replaced by a piece of cardboard. Mr. Krum stopped right in front of the house and turned the car off. Was this where he lived?

"Please get out of the vehicle."

Jack and I climbed out one side while Mr. Krum climbed out the other and then circled around behind us.

"Please walk into the house."

We started walking. Jack grabbed the screen door and it practically came off in his hand. Only the top hinge was holding it in place.

"Nice place you have here," he muttered.

"It is sufficient. Please proceed."

Jack pushed open the solid wooden door and we walked in. It was immediately apparent that Mr. Krum didn't live here. Nobody lived here. There were a few crates and a broken chair, but nothing else.

"Through the door to your right, please," he said, motioning with the pistol.

"All this politeness would be a lot nicer if you weren't pointing a gun at us," Jack grumbled as he started to walk.

"There is no reason why this cannot be done politely. I simply need you to answer my questions."

Jack pushed through a swinging door and I followed. I had an urge to throw the door back at Mr. Krum, the way they would have done in some sort of gangster movie, but I didn't. I just followed Jack into the room, the kitchen. There was a table and six chairs. The counter was covered with dirty dishes, and there was an icebox and a wood-burning stove, its stone chimney reaching up through the ceiling.

"Sit . . . please."

Jack took a seat and I sat down on the chair right beside him. It creaked and slumped as I settled into it, and for an instant I thought it was going to give way and collapse. It was wooden and old and badly in need of repair.

Mr. Krum pulled a chair over and turned it backwards. He sat down with his arms and the pistol resting on the back of the chair. Then he looked at his watch.

"There is little time, and I need my questions answered."

"We have answered your questions," Jack told him stubbornly.

"No, you have avoided answering my questions, and I think that is not wise. Your choices are to provide me with answers or be questioned by my associates."

Jack and I exchanged a look.

"Did you think I was working alone?"

"We hadn't thought of anything," I said.

"Please do not deny that you had some suspicions. It was obvious from your refusal to answer my questions, the manner in which you tried to avoid me, and the way George would chew on the inside of his cheek . . . as he's doing now."

I stopped myself.

"I simply need answers. I have no desire to hurt either of you boys. But if I do not get answers, I am certain that my associates will be neither as patient nor as concerned as I for your well-being."

"What will happen to us if we tell you what you want to know?" Jack demanded. "You can't afford to let us go free."

"If you co-operate you will be left here, tied up. A call will be made tomorrow to inform the police of your whereabouts."

"And then we'll tell them everything about you," Jack said. "You'll be arrested . . . but you know that."

"I would expect nothing less."

"You don't care if they arrest you?" I wanted to know.

"Alas, I will not be here to be taken into custody."

"So that means whatever you're doing is going to be done before tomorrow," I reasoned.

He nodded his head, and a slight smile came to his lips. "I was certain that you would make a first-class newspaperman."

"What are you going to do?"

"Do you really think he'll tell us?" Jack said.

Mr. Krum shrugged. "You will not be able to tell anybody until long after the plan is completed, so I will share it with you. Tonight, at ten-thirty, there will be a simultaneous attack on the German prisoner-of-war camp in Bowmanville and the D.I.L. plant."

"The D.I.L. plant! But our mother is . . ." I let the sentence trail off. I didn't have to worry. She'd be home by five, and safe. Home and looking for us.

"Your mother is working the day shift today," Mr. Krum said.

"How do you know that?" Jack demanded.

"I know the rotation of her shifts as I know many things. I was hoping, for your sakes, that she would not be present at the time of the attack."

"Why . . . why does that matter?" Jack asked anxiously.

"I would not wish anything to happen to her. You are both fine boys . . . I like both of you."

"But if you're attacking those other places, why did you want to know all about the camp?" I asked.

"Ahh . . . that is the next stage of the plan. These sites are being attacked merely to attract attention. The men training at the camp will be drawn off in both directions to offer assistance. It is at that time that the camp itself will be attacked."

"What's the point in doing that?" Jack asked.

"The camp has been host to a number of very important persons. Tonight, one of the most important men in the Allied forces is there."

My eyes widened slightly and I turned to Jack. Was he was after Little Bill?

"From your expressions, it appears that you have some knowledge of the person to whom I'm referring," Mr. Krum said.

I tried to make my face go blank. Had we given something away . . . had he overheard us talking?

"That information, as is much information, is known to me through radio transmissions. All those men who consider themselves master spies, and they cannot keep secrets . . . I know *everything*."

I had no idea how much information he had discovered, but I knew that they didn't even suspect him. I'd been told that if they thought he was a spy they would have arrested him. His cover as a newspaper editor had worked perfectly.

"It doesn't matter what you think you know!" Jack snapped defiantly. "That place is well defended."

"And how would you know that?"

"I'm not telling you anything. You just try to break in there and see what happens to you!"

"I will not be the only one attacking. There are three special teams each with six elite agents."

"And you're their leader?" I asked.

Mr. Krum laughed. "Far from that. I am simply a loyal citizen."

"A traitor is what you are!" Jack snapped.

"Hardly. To fail to act in the defence of my country would be to behave as a traitor."

"But you told us you were a Canadian," I protested.

"I am Canadian by declaration, but German by birth."

"You're nothing but a stinking Nazi!" Jack practically yelled.

"I suggest that you use neither that tone nor the insult when my associates arrive. As I have said, they are less tolerant than I." He paused. "I am a German. I am loyal to Germany . . . loyal to all my family that remain in that country. When I was contacted, there was no question where my allegiance lay."

"What about all those things you said about the Nazis being evil?" I asked.

"Simply a way to cover myself. Always look for the one who protests loudest to be the one who is hiding the most."

"But you even tried to enlist in the army . . . why would you do that?"

"Can you not imagine what service I would have been to the German government if I could have become part of Canadian intelligence or communications?" he asked. "But enough talk."

Mr. Krum stood up. He went to a cupboard, opened it up and pulled out a long coil of rope.

"For the safety of us all, it is best that you boys be tied up. I would not wish to have you attempt to escape. The results would be *most* unpleasant."

He put the gun down on the counter and opened a drawer. I gasped slightly as he pulled out a long knife. Sunlight caught the blade and it glittered. He bent down and placed it on the floor. Then with his foot slid it toward me. It stopped just a few feet short of my chair. He took the coil of rope and tossed it so that it also landed right by my feet.

"George, you are to tie up your brother."

"I'm . . . I'm not going to do that," I stammered, shaking my head.

"You will do as you are told. I will direct you."

I hesitated.

"Now!" he barked.

"Do what he says, George," Jack told me.

I bent over and picked up the rope and then the knife. Mr. Krum directed me to loop the rope around both my brother and the back of the chair, then cut it. The knife sliced easily through the thick cord rope. I was amazed by how sharp it was.

"Now cut three more pieces . . . smaller . . . perhaps two feet in length."

Reluctantly I did what I was told.

"Secure each of your brother's legs to a leg of the chair."

I looped the piece around Jack's leg and started to tie it. I looked up at him apologetically.

"Tighter! Much tighter!" Mr. Krum ordered.

"Sorry," I mouthed to Jack as I pulled the rope much more tightly around him.

I finished the first leg and then did the same with the second, snugging the rope in but leaving it as loose as I dared. Next I tied his hands together behind the back of the chair.

Mr. Krum came over. He was still holding the pistol in one hand but with the other he proceeded to check each loop of rope. Then he stepped back.

"Cut three more pieces of similar length," he ordered.

I knew without asking that I was now going to cut the ropes that would hold me. I did what I was told. Each time the knife sliced easily through the cord.

"Now sit," he said. "I want you to tie both of your legs in the same manner you secured your brother's."

I reached out and took the first piece of rope. If it was strange to tie up my brother, this was completely unreal. I pulled the rope until my leg was pressed tightly against the leg of the chair. I put a knot in the end and then double-knotted it. I did the same with the second leg.

"Now put your hands behind your back . . .behind the back of the chair."

I did what I was told, and Mr. Krum circled around behind me. He bent down. I heard the sound of the gun being placed on the floor and then felt the rope being looped around my wrists. It hurt as he tightened it, and I pulled away.

"I am sorry, but I cannot loosen it," Mr. Krum said.

When he'd finished, he draped a coil of rope around my chest so that my back was pressed against the back of the chair. He then dropped to his knees and tightened the knots on both of my legs, pulling them until they hurt. Satisfied, he went to Jack and tightened every rope in turn. Any hope that I'd left some slack was gone.

"Now we may begin to—"

He stopped at the sound of tires against gravel. There was a car pulling up. My first thought was that somebody was coming who would rescue us, and then I remembered that Mr. Krum was expecting the rest of his party to arrive. There was the sound of a car door slamming, and then another and another and another. There were a number of people. It had to be the team of "elite" agents he'd mentioned—Nazis. And they were coming here to talk to us. I couldn't help but think about something we'd said just before the Lieutenant-Colonel asked us to sign the secrecy oaths—how we wouldn't even tell what we knew . . . even if we were tortured by Nazi agents. Brave words.

# CHAPTER SEVENTEEN

THE BACK DOOR OPENED and a man strode through. *"Guten Tag, Herr Krum. Wie geht's—"*

He stopped in his tracks as he saw us. He looked shocked, his mouth hanging open, speechless. A second man stopped behind him.

*"Was sind diese Leute?"* the first man demanded angrily. *"Warum sind Die hier?"*

"I had no choice but to—"

*"Nein, nein, nein. Nur in Deutsch."*

*"Ja, ja."*

The man came completely into the room and five other men followed him in. The first man continued to ask Mr. Krum questions. He was angry and upset, and Mr. Krum was stammering in response. He looked worried.

I caught a few of the words—words I knew from my grandparents—but there was no way I could make any sense of anything. I wondered if Jack understood better. He knew a few more words than I did.

The man who was obviously in charge came over and stood before us.

"I am told that you have important information," he said crisply.

"You speak English," I said.

"I speak many languages. English is just one. I am going to now ask you boys some questions and I expect answers."

"We're not going to—"

Suddenly he reached out and slapped Jack across the face! His chair rocked backwards with the blow!

"Leave him alone!" I screamed.

He turned to me. "Would you rather I strike you?"

"No . . . no," I stammered.

"Wise. Answer my questions and there will be no further need to strike anybody. Now, tell me of your involvement with the camp."

"We don't know much," I said. "We've been around it a couple of times and—"

"Don't tell him anything!" Jack yelled at me.

The man reached out again and slapped my brother across the face, harder this time. I cringed and looked away. My eyes fell on Mr. Krum. He was cringing too.

The man was now holding Jack's face in his hands and squeezing. Jack was trying to look away, to move his head, but it was hopeless.

"You will tell us what we want to know. It may be slow and painful or it may be without pain, but you will tell. Do you understand?" he yelled.

Jack continued to struggle, and I could see the man tightening his grip until my brother's face was distorted in pain.

"Just stop!" I shouted out. "I'll talk to you . . . I'll tell you everything."

He released Jack's face and came and stood right beside me. "If you do not tell me, it may be necessary for me to take other measures."

"What do you mean?"

"Do you live with your parents?"

"Just our mother, because . . . why . . . why do you want to know?"

"It would be a simple matter to send two of my men to retrieve her. If you do not give me the information I require, that will happen. Do you want your mother to be our prisoner as well?"

"I told you I'd tell you everything!" I protested.

"That is my, how do you say . . . insurance policy. At the first lie I will dispatch my men to get your mother."

"I'll tell you everything!" Jack yelled. "I'll tell you everything!"

He turned to Jack. "*You* will tell us nothing."

What did he mean?"

"You will remain quiet, not uttering a word, while your brother talks. From him I expect the truth. From you I expect only half-truths. It is better for everybody that I get nothing but the truth."

"I'll do that . . . I'll tell you everything . . . just please leave my brother alone . . . please!" I begged.

"Fine. Let us begin. Tell me about the camp. I wish to know about the guards, the paths, and the manner in which you entered the grounds. Do you understand?"

"I'll tell you everything."

"Excellent. Let us begin."

"That is the last question. You were wise not to resist or to lie," he said.

I felt my whole body relax as he walked away at last. It was over . . . he was going to leave me alone . . . he wasn't going to hurt our mother. But what now?

I looked over at my brother. I wanted some reassurance that everything was going to be okay. Instead I found myself gawking at him. His face was swollen and bloody and he stared vacantly at the floor. He looked as if he was in shock.

The man walked across the room and I watched as he stopped in front of one of the others. Mr. Krum stood off to the side. The remaining four were nowhere to be seen.

"May I get them some water?" Mr. Krum asked.

The man turned around. "*Ja, ja,* that is fine."

Mr. Krum took two glasses down from a cupboard. He went to a pump on the counter and began working it. At first nothing came from it but a high-pitched squeak as he moved the handle up and down. Then a trickle of brown liquid emerged, followed by a lot more, and finally clear water started to run into the sink. He filled the two glasses and brought one to Jack, holding it up to his lips. Jack turned away.

"I don't want it," Jack spat. "I don't want anything from you."

"Do not be silly. This may be the last drink you have until tomorrow, when somebody comes to find you. You will need water."

"Take it, Jack," I quietly pleaded.

It wasn't just that I wanted him to drink, but that I knew I couldn't if he didn't. It was bad enough that I was the one who'd done most of the talking. He turned his head back toward Mr. Krum. As he opened his mouth he cringed in pain. He allowed Mr. Krum to pour the liquid into his mouth and gulped it down, a trickle slipping around the glass and down his chin.

Mr. Krum brought me the second glass. I drank the water greedily and it slid down my throat. It had a funny taste but it was still the best water I'd ever had in my life.

"Thanks," I mumbled.

"It is the least I could do," he said quietly. "You were wise to give them the information. These are not men to fool with."

I nodded. I had told them most of what we knew . . . but not everything. I'd told them about Corbett's Creek, but not about the waterfall. I'd told them about the guards in the jeeps, but not about those men I'd seen walking around the grounds. And when they asked questions about the buildings,

I hadn't really been sure about where some of the things were.

"What happens now?" I asked.

"Nothing," Mr. Krum replied. "We will leave soon and get into position for the attacks."

"And us?"

"You remain. A call will be made tomorrow. I will make it myself and let them know of your location. Your mother must already be concerned."

"What time is it?" I asked.

He looked at his watch. "Almost eight o'clock."

"She'll be really worried."

"I wish there was some way I could let her know that you will be safe, but there is not."

"And you?"

"And me what?" Mr. Krum asked.

"What happens to you?"

"I will be leaving with the agents. All of us will be leaving."

"By submarine?" I asked.

He looked taken aback by my question. "That would be the way to leave."

*"Herr Krum!"* called out the leader.

He turned around.

*"Lassen Sie allein!"* he barked.

"I have to leave," Mr. Krum told us.

He walked over to the two men, and then all three of them exited the room, leaving Jack and me alone.

"Are you all right?" Jack whispered.

"I'm okay. You?"

"My jaw is sore, but I'm okay."

It looked more than just sore. The whole side of his face was swollen. I'd never seen anything like that before.

"You didn't have any choice," Jack whispered.

"What?" I asked.

"You didn't have any choice but to talk to them."

"I guess not."

"And you told them just enough," he whispered, his voice just barely audible. "Let them go in Corbett's Creek and they'll be caught for sure."

From the other room came loud voices, so loud that if I'd understood more German I'd have known what they were arguing about.

"Sounds like somebody isn't so happy," I said.

"If I weren't in these ropes I'd try and make them all unhappy."

The voices in the other room faded away and Mr. Krum reappeared in the doorway. He did look very unhappy . . . no, not unhappy . . . scared. He walked into the kitchen and from behind him I heard the sound of the front door opening up and then a few seconds later closing.

"We . . . we . . . are leaving now," he said, his voice breaking over the last few words.

"Can you please call our mother tonight . . . just to tell her we're okay?" I pleaded.

"Not tonight," he said shaking his head. "Not tomorrow."

"But you promised!"

He shook his head again. He looked pale, and I was positive he was shaking.

"Why won't you call her?" Jack demanded.

"I cannot . . . I am not allowed."

"But if you don't call, nobody will know to come and find us!"

"I am sorry . . . most sorry . . . I was told that I should not have brought you here. And since it was my mistake, I must correct it myself."

"What do you mean, correct it?" I gasped, my voice barely above a whisper.

"I am most sorry, boys. Most sorry."

He reached into his jacket and removed his pistol. He aimed it at Jack's head.

# CHAPTER EIGHTEEN

"YOU CAN'T DO THIS, Mr. Krum," I gasped. "You can't!" I pressed myself against the back of the chair, as if somehow that would save or protect me.

"They fear what would happen . . . if . . . if you escaped or were discovered. I told them you would not be found here until it was too late. But . . . but they did not wish to take a chance."

"We wouldn't tell anybody, even if they found us!"

He lowered the pistol. "Please do not make promises that you would not keep. I have no choice."

In the background I heard the sound of an engine starting. They were leaving.

"Look away, please," he said softly.

"No, I won't!" Jack snapped defiantly. "I'm going to look right at you."

"It would be less difficult."

"Less difficult for you!"

I started to bite the inside of my cheek, but stopped. I didn't want him to see that. I wasn't going to give him that satisfaction.

Mr. Krum raised the gun and walked another step closer to Jack. Jack thrashed about in his ropes, desperately trying to free himself. I couldn't bear to watch . . . I looked away and closed my eyes tightly. An explosion—a shot! And then there was a second and a third and a fourth. I opened my eyes, terrified. Mr. Krum was standing with the smoking gun in his hand. He had one finger held in front of his mouth and Jack was still there . . . still alive . . . staring, wide-eyed.

"Not a sound," Mr. Krum whispered. "Not now and not until you are sure we are all gone. If they return to the house and they find you alive they will kill you both . . . and me as well."

He turned and walked to the door. Suddenly he stopped and turned back around.

"I am a good German. We do not kill children or women."

Before I could even think of answering he was gone. I heard his feet move quickly across the floor, the door opening and then closing. Within a few seconds I heard two car doors slam, another engine start and then the sound of tires against gravel as they left. Finally there was silence.

"I think they're gone," I croaked.

Jack whimpered in response. Despite being tied into the chair he was still shaking violently.

"Are you all right?"

He didn't answer.

"Jack! Are you all right?"

He nodded his head ever so slightly and I could see the tears flowing down his cheeks. I couldn't remember ever seeing Jack cry.

"He . . . he had it pointed right at my face . . . I was looking down the barrel . . . and then he shot . . . there," Jack said, motioning with his chin.

Just off to the side I could see four holes in the wall, the places where the bullets had hit.

"He made it sound like he'd killed us," I said. "So they could hear the shots outside."

"I could feel the bullets pass by . . . the heat and the smell . . . I thought I was dead," he sobbed.

"But we're okay."

Jack shook his head. "We're not okay."

"Sure we are, they're gone and we just wait until somebody comes to get us."

"Who will get us?" he hissed.

"Mom or the police or . . ."

I suddenly realized that they'd only come if they were called, and now Mr. Krum would not be free to call anybody. He couldn't very well excuse himself to make a call to free two people he'd killed.

"We have to get away or we'll starve to death, or die of thirst."

"Somebody will come."

"Out here, way off the highway, miles out of town?" Jack demanded.

"Then . . . then we have to get out of these ropes ourselves."

"I could have slipped out of the ropes you tied, but then Krum tightened them so much that I can't move at all."

"Then we have to use something to cut them." I looked around. "The back window is broken. How about a piece of glass from that?"

"That wouldn't work. What we need is a knife or . . . hey, where is the knife he used to cut the rope?" Jack asked.

We both turned to the counter. There it was, still sitting there, the sharp blade shining brightly.

"If I can just get close to it, maybe I can knock it off somehow," Jack said.

He started to use the very tips of his toes to inch the chair forward. I watched as he made painfully slow progress across the kitchen, bit by bit. He finally clunked his legs right up against the counter.

"What do you do now?" I asked.

"I've got to somehow rock myself so I can lean up on the counter . . . maybe I can reach it with my head and knock it closer, or even onto the floor."

"But even if you can do that, what good would it do?" I asked.

"I don't know. Maybe we can use it somehow to cut the ropes on our feet."

"That still wouldn't get our hands free," I pointed out.

"But if our feet were free we could walk out to the highway."

"I don't know . . ."

"You got any better ideas?" Jack demanded. "We can't just do nothing and wait here to die!"

I shook my head. "I can't think of anything."

"Then just sit there and let me take care of things."

Jack pushed up on his toes and the front legs of the chair rose off the ground. He flattened his feet and the chair rocked forward. He did the same again, rising a little bit more, and it rocked even farther forward. Again and again he bucked and rocked, and each time he seemed to get higher.

"Just a little bit more," he grunted.

He rocked backwards and—

"Aaaaahhhh!" Jack yelled as he fell over, landing on the floor with a thundering crash!

"Jack, are you okay?" I yelled.

"I'm okay . . . I smashed up my hands, but I'm okay . . . I think . . . but there's no way I can get up."

He rolled back and forth, rocking on his back, and then tipped onto his side.

"If you can knock the knife down here I think I can get it now . . . it might even be better that I fell down . . . if you can get the knife."

"But if you couldn't get it, how can I do it?"

"I don't know. You're lighter. Maybe it'll be easier. In any case, you have to try."

"But what if I tip over too, like you?"

"Just don't."

"But if I do?" I asked.

"Then we'll be in even deeper than we are now. We'll be as dead as if he'd shot us."

I took a big breath. Jack was right, there was no choice. I used my toes the same way I'd seen Jack do it. I was surprised by how easily I could move. Maybe there was more play in the ropes looped around my feet. As I inched forward the chair creaked noisily. I crossed over to the counter, just beside Jack. He looked up.

"You can do it, George."

I wasn't as confident as he sounded. Slowly I raised myself up on my toes and rocked backwards. My stomach rolled forward as I went back. I could perfectly picture in my mind toppling over like Jack. I let go and rocked forward.

"Do it again!" Jack ordered.

I pushed up on my toes and then let go and I rocked forward . . . and onto my feet. I was all bent over and the chair was on my back in the air.

"That's great!" Jack exclaimed. "Can you throw yourself up onto the counter?"

"I'm not sure," I said. The chair creaked and twisted under me. It sounded as if the whole thing might just fall apart. Maybe there was another way.

"I'm going to try something else," I announced.

"What? What are you going to try?"

"Watch."

I shuffled around so that I was facing away from the counter. Carefully I took a little hop, moving forward on both feet at the same time. This was definitely a faster way of moving.

"What are you doing?" Jack demanded. "You have to get the knife!"

I looked back. He was arching his neck, trying desperately to watch me.

"I'm not going to try to cut the ropes. I think I can smash the chair that's holding the ropes instead."

I hopped again and again and again, until I was right in front of the stove's stone chimney. It was rough-hewn rock and it stuck out from the wall. Slowly I turned around so that I was facing completely away from it. Then I shuffled backwards until I could feel the bottom spindle of the chair pressed up against it.

"What are you doing?" Jack yelled.

I took a little hop forward, away from the chimney.

*Here goes,* I said to myself, and then hopped backwards with all my strength.

The chair thudded up against the brick. I wiggled all over. Was it any looser at all? I couldn't tell. I moved forward again and then threw myself backwards, and the bottom spindle hit against the stone.

"Is it working?" Jack asked anxiously.

"I'm not sure."

I flexed my leg muscles trying to force them farther apart. I could feel the chair giving ever so slightly, the legs bowing out a little. One more try. I moved farther out from the wall and then hopped twice backwards and there was a tremendous crack! I looked over my shoulder and down—one of the spindles had broken in two!

"It's through! I've broken the bottom spindle!" I yelled.

"Great, keep going!"

If I could break the side spindles as well, then maybe all the legs would just fall off. I turned to the side. Hopping sideways and throwing myself into the chimney would be harder, but I thought I could do it. I tried to turn when I felt myself going backwards. My whole weight fell onto the back legs of the chair and they shot sideways. I felt myself tumbling over. I braced myself for the fall . . . and—

"Uggggg!" I screamed as I landed with a tremendous crash.

"George! George!"

"I'm okay. I fell over . . . but my feet are free!" I yelled.

The parts from the bottom of the chair—legs and spindles and seat—were scattered around me. My feet were in loops of rope still tied to the legs but they were completely free to move. Unfortunately my hands were still tied behind me to the upper spindles.

"Can you get up?" Jack asked.

"I'll try." I rolled onto my side and pushed off so I was on my knees, and then I struggled to my feet, the legs of the chair jutting into me.

"I'm up. I just have to get my hands free."

I moved over and rammed myself backward into the chimney again. The jolt registered throughout my entire body. I did it again and heard a crack. Again and again and again, and then two of the spindles dropped to the ground. I furiously wriggled my hands and the ropes got even looser as other pieces of the chair fell, until finally there was nothing else. I walked over to Jack, my hands free of the chair but still tied behind my back.

"I can get the knife now, I'm pretty sure," I said, towering over him.

I backed up to the counter and awkwardly jumped up onto it. It groaned and gave way slightly, and for a second I thought it was going to collapse under my weight. I looked backward to the knife and reached out until I could feel the blade against my fingers. I pushed it around slightly so I could grab it by the handle.

"I've got it, Jack! I've got it."

"Can you bring it down here?"

"I'm not sure, but I figure it would be better if I just kept it here. I think I can cut myself free."

Carefully I moved my fingers along the handle until I was holding it right where it met the blade. I shifted it more into the fingers of my right hand and pressed the blade forward until I was sure it was touching the rope. Then I started moving my hand, slowly, hoping the edge of the knife was cutting into the fibre of the rope.

"Is it working?" Jack asked.

"I can't see, but I think it is. It must be."

I doubled my efforts. My hand was starting to hurt from the exertion and—

"Occhh!" I yelled as I dropped the knife to the counter.

"What happened?"

"I cut myself with the knife!"

"Are you okay?"

"I can't see . . . I can feel where it cut in." I could also feel my hands getting wet . . . was that my blood? "If I turn around, can you look?"

"I can't see anything from here. Besides, we haven't got any time," Jack said. "It's getting late. It looks like the sun is almost down."

I looked across the kitchen and out the window. It was getting darker. The sun was just peeking out from between some trees. It wouldn't be long until it set. That had to make it after nine o'clock . . . maybe later. And if it was going to be hard finding help now, I could only imagine how much more difficult it would be in the dark, miles away from anything or anyone we knew.

I felt around with my fingers until I found the knife again. I grabbed it and carefully moved it forward until I had it where I wanted it. At least I'd already cut partway through the rope . . . assuming I could start cutting in the same place again. I transferred the knife to my left hand and felt around with the fingers of my right to try to find the cut. I moved my finger up until I discovered a spot that was frayed. Could I move the knife over to my right hand and still keep track of where it was? I tried to picture it all in my mind as I transferred it over. I started sawing away at the rope, this time pulling my left hand away to try to avoid cutting it again. I strained against the ropes and—my hands popped free!

"I did it, Jack! I did it!"

"Help me up . . . please, help me!"

I climbed off the counter and dropped to his side. I was just going to start cutting when I glanced down at my left hand. There was a long, nasty-looking gash and blood flowed freely from it.

"Come on, George, what are you waiting for?"

"I'm . . . sorry, let me just get my legs free."

Quickly I cut the ropes holding my legs to the remnants of the chair. I then grabbed Jack by the shoulders and lifted. He was heavy, and I wasn't sure if I could do it. I groaned as I heaved him upright, with the legs of the chair back on the floor.

"Cut the ropes."

I reached back, grabbed the knife from the counter and slipped it into the loop of rope holding his wrists. The blade bit into the cord and sliced through it effortlessly. It snapped, and Jack pulled his hands free.

"That feels so good," he said.

"Here, you can cut the others," I said, offering him the knife.

"Can't," he said shaking his head. "My wrist . . ."

Even in the last fading rays of light I could see that his right wrist was swollen to twice the size of the other.

"I hurt it when I fell. I think it might be broken," Jack said. He cradled the injured wrist in the other hand. "Can you cut me free?"

I bent down and cut the two ropes holding him to the chair. Jack staggered to his feet unsteadily.

"Do you know what time it is?" he asked.

"The sun sets about nine-thirty."

"That gives us about an hour until the attacks take place. We have to get help."

"But what about your wrist . . . and my hand?"

"We'll wrap something around your hand to stop the bleeding."

"And your wrist?"

"Nothing . . . we'll do nothing. It'll have to wait. Let's just get out of here."

"I never want to see this place again in my life," I said.

"Can you get the door?" Jack asked.

I pulled it open and started to walk out.

"Wait a second." Jack suddenly stopped in his tracks. "Take one more look back."

I strained my eyes to see the outline of the features of the dingy little kitchen. What did he want me to see?

"That was almost the last thing either of us ever saw . . . just think about it for a second." He paused and let his words sink in.

"Now, let's go."

# CHAPTER NINETEEN

THE MOON WAS FULL and peeking out between the trees as we stumbled up the farm lane back toward the highway. Jack stumbled and groaned in pain. I knew his arm had to hurt badly . . . at least just judging from how much the cut on my hand was stinging. Then there was his face—it looked worse than his arm. I tripped in a pothole and almost fell over myself.

"Be careful," Jack warned as he reached out with his good hand and grabbed me before I tumbled.

"It's hard to walk . . . the road is in pretty bad shape."

"We'll be at the highway soon."

"And then what are we going to do?"

"We'll try and flag down a car," Jack said, as confidently as he could.

"I can't wait to get home. Mom is going to be so worried."

"There isn't time to go home."

"But—?"

"Mom will just have to stay worried a little bit longer. We have to get to the camp. We have to tell them about the other attacks and warn them that they're the real target, or at least that somebody at the camp is."

Up ahead a flash of light—a passing car—showed how much farther we had to go.

"Maybe we can speed up," I suggested.

"My legs are still shaky and I don't want to risk falling . . . my wrist is really hurting. It throbs every time my heart beats. How's your hand?"

I looked down. Even in the dim light I could see that the whole back of my hand was covered in sticky, drying blood.

"It's almost stopped bleeding," I said.

"I wish we had something to wrap around it," Jack said.

"I wish we had a sling for your arm," I answered.

The highway was getting closer and closer. We'd soon be there and—I was struck by a thought.

"Jack, do you think somebody could be waiting for us out there?"

"You mean like they left a guard or something?"

"Yeah."

"You don't guard dead men. They think we're dead. They're all getting in position for their attack."

"Not them," I said. "Somebody else. Mr. Krum said there were lots of people like him."

"Krum was just talking, either to scare us or maybe so he wouldn't feel so much like a rat and a traitor," Jack said.

We stopped at the highway. There were no cars visible in either direction. It was dark and quiet.

"Which way do we go?"

"The plant is to the right, and the town and the entrance to the camp are to the left."

"Which is closer?"

"I'm not completely sure, but I think the plant. It was hard to tell from the floor of the car."

"Maybe we should go there and ask Mr. Granger to call the camp."

"That might work . . . but what if we run into somebody?"

"I thought we *wanted* to run into somebody."

"I meant some of the Nazis. They're going there to attack the plant. What if they see us coming?"

"You're right." I paused. "But they're also going to attack the camp. Either way there's a chance."

"The attack on the camp is later. Maybe we can get there before they move into position. We should just try to flag down anything that comes in either direction."

We started down the road, travelling right down the centre line. It wasn't as if there was a danger of anything sneaking up on us.

"Something's coming," Jack called out.

I stopped and listened. In the dark I could hear the distant sound of something moving. Then two headlights appeared around a curve in the road behind us. It got louder and louder as it closed in. It was a truck—a truck headed toward the camp.

"Hey!" Jack yelled. He tried to jump up and down, but he grimaced in pain and grabbed his injured hand.

"Stop!" I yelled, waving my hands in the air.

The truck barrelled down on us. It got bigger and bigger and bigger and—

"Get out of the way!" Jack screamed.

We both scrambled as the truck swooshed by between us, sending a burst of hot air and gravel into our faces. It hadn't even slowed down, and the red taillights soon receded into the distance.

"It was like he didn't even see us!" I exclaimed.

"I think that truck was from the D.I.L. plant. Even if he saw us he's not allowed to stop, for security reasons," Jack said. "Remember?"

"Maybe we should walk on the shoulder," I suggested.

"We're okay to walk on the road . . . just don't stand there when something's coming. What time do you think it is?"

"I'm not sure, but it's got to be close to ten by now."

"We have to hurry . . . do you think you could go faster without me?"

"I guess I could, but . . . I'm not going anywhere without you!" I protested. "We're sticking together."

At least part of the reason for that was because there was no way I was going to be out there by myself.

"Then we may have to try a shortcut," Jack said.

"Where do you see a shortcut?"

"That way." Jack pointed off to the forest.

"Through the woods?"

"I think we're almost right on top of the camp."

"Are you sure?"

"We left the town and headed west. I didn't hear the sound

of us crossing over any bridges, so I think we're still east of Corbett's Creek. And if we are—"

"Then the camp is just to the south of us. Do you think we can find our way in the dark?"

"We might bumble and stumble around a bit . . . I just hope I don't fall on my wrist."

"I'm more worried that we'll get turned around and end up going in a big circle."

"So, we'll just keep the moon to our left and we'll be okay."

"No matter what, we won't be able to move very quietly."

"But we don't *want* to move quietly."

"We don't?"

"We're not trying to sneak into the camp. We want to warn them. So the faster we find a guard, the faster we'll be able to tell them about what's happening."

That made perfect sense. It also made it seem so much more possible. All we had to do was stumble in the general direction of the camp and make enough noise that the guards would find us. Judging from how hard it was to sneak in, that couldn't be too difficult at all. Still, I didn't want to head into the forest at night.

"Something's coming!" Jack shouted.

Up ahead lights appeared. The vehicle was coming from the direction we wanted to go, but that didn't matter. If we could flag it down we could still avoid a trip through the dark woods.

The lights got brighter as it got nearer. Judging from their size, it was a car.

"Let's make sure this one at least sees us," Jack said.

He walked off the shoulder and into the lane of the oncoming car. Reluctantly I followed, remembering how the big truck had just missed us.

"Wave your hands!" Jack yelled.

I started to jump up and down and wave my arms in the air. The lights were coming closer and I had to fight the urge to run off the road and back onto the shoulder. But this was our last chance before we had to head into the bush. Jack began to yell, and I yelled too.

The car seemed to be slowing down . . . or was I just hoping it was? Yes, it was! It was definitely slowing down! I heard the rumble of gravel as it pulled over on to the shoulder.

"It's stopping! It's stopping!" I yelled.

It pulled completely off the road, came to a stop right in front of us and—it was a police car! The door opened and out popped Chief Smith!

I was stunned. Why was he here?

"I've been looking for you boys!" he exclaimed.

My mind raced in different directions. He was the chief of police, so of course he knew we were missing and would be out to find us. But how did he happen along right here. . . ? Unless he was coming to the deserted farmhouse because he *knew* . . . he knew we were in the farmhouse because he was one of *them*.

"You're in big trouble!" he exclaimed. "Into the car, right now!"

I looked over at Jack, searching for some sign to tell me

what to do. His eyes were wide open—at least the one not starting to swell shut.

"Jack?" I asked softly.

He turned to me.

"What do we do?"

He looked back at the Chief, who was now walking toward us, and then to me. "Run," he hissed.

I burst off the road, taking a step in one direction before realizing that Jack was running across the road in the other. I skidded around and raced after him.

"Wait!" yelled the Chief. "Stop!"

I raced down the shoulder of the road, almost tumbling onto my face as I hit the ditch at the bottom, and scrambled up the other side. I braced myself, waiting for the sound of a bullet and the searing pain as it entered my back. Instead, tree branches smacked into me, stinging my face, as I broke into the cover of the forest.

"Come back!" the Chief yelled.

I staggered forward, desperately trying to gain some ground in the pitch black. I tripped and landed heavily on the forest floor with something hard sticking into my side. Then I scrambled forward on all fours, not knowing where I was going but certain I needed to get farther from the road. Finally my hands slipped out from under me and I fell into a puddle of shallow water. I raised my head and didn't move. I just listened. There was no sound. Not the noise of somebody coming after me, no sounds of the forest, not even the sound of breathing . . . I realized I was holding my breath.

"Listen to me, boys!" the Chief's voice bellowed out. "I didn't mean to scare you! Come on back to the road. I need to get you home to your mother! She's worried sick about you!"

I'd forgotten all about Mom. She had to be scared to death wondering what had happened to us.

"Whatever mischief you boys have gotten into can't be that bad! You come out now and everything will be forgotten. I'll just drive you home . . . okay?"

I *did* want to go home . . . and he sounded sincere. Maybe we'd just overreacted. And he'd be able to warn them at the camp. He wasn't a spy . . . just because his family had once come from Germany. So had ours! Besides, if he was a spy I was sure that the people at the camp would have known— and yet they hadn't known about Mr. Krum.

I looked all around me in the dark. Somewhere out there, maybe just a dozen feet away, was Jack. He'd know what we should do.

"Come on, boys, we can't wait here all night . . . don't make me come in there and get you. Then I *will* be mad!"

That sealed it for me. I wasn't going back to the road, and I couldn't just wait there, in case he did come after us. I slowly rose to my feet. I was just going to keep moving farther into the forest, farther away from the Chief. I took a few steps and then froze. That also meant I was probably moving farther away from my brother.

I turned my head away from the road. "Jack!" I hissed. There was no answer.

"Jack!" I called out, louder.

"What was that?" Obviously the Chief had heard me. "Are you trying to find your way out? I'll keep talking so you can come toward my voice!"

I caught a glimpse of the moon through the trees. Jack had said we should just keep moving and keep the moon on our left and we'd be able to find the camp. I started to walk slowly, the moon over my left shoulder, the Chief's booming voice directly behind me. I'd keep moving away quietly and then stop and call out for Jack when I was farther from the road and safe.

It wasn't long before the Chief's voice started to fade. I kept moving until I couldn't hear him at all. Either I'd put enough space between us, or he'd stopped calling—or both. The trees started to thin out, and without the canopy above me more light was hitting the forest floor to brighten my path. Up ahead I could see that the trees and bush gave way completely to an open field. Was this the camp? No, it couldn't be . . . I hadn't hit the railroad embankment yet. The embankment—that was what would guide me! Once I hit the embankment I'd simply follow the tracks until I hit one of the culverts and then head along the road!

I stopped at the edge of the field, which was bathed in the bright moonlight. It would be easy to see my way, but I would also be visible to anybody as I crossed the field. That could be good—if it was Jack who was looking for me—or bad. There were other people heading for the camp too, people I never wanted to see again. Either way, I couldn't stay there.

I'd just taken my first step into the field when I heard some sounds off to the side. I swivelled my head to look but I couldn't see anything. The sound continued. Somebody or something was moving through the bush. Slowly I lowered myself to the ground and took shelter in the knee-high grass. Whatever it was, it was coming closer. I flattened myself until only the very top of my head protruded out of the grass. As long as I stayed perfectly still, perfectly quiet, I knew that something could practically bump right into me without seeing me. I just—

"Jack!" I screamed, jumping up from my hiding spot. I ran over and threw my arms around him. "I was so scared, and—"

"Be quiet, you little idiot!" he hissed. "He's right behind us!"

"Who?"

"The Chief," he whispered. "He's coming after us through the trees."

I turned my head in the direction we'd both just come. There was the unmistakable sound of somebody else breaking through the underbrush.

"Can you run?" Jack asked.

"Sure . . . of course."

"Good. We have to get across the field before he gets this far."

We started to run. The ground was level and flat and we were moving fast, the grass swishing against our legs. I looked back over my shoulder. The edge of the forest was black. We wouldn't be able to see anybody coming out of the trees, but I was positive that they would still see us.

Up ahead the far edge of the field was looming, and beyond that it simply looked black—as black as the forest on the other side. I tried to pick out individual images—a gap between the trees, rocks, an opening we could head for, something—but it remained just a dark blur stretching out of sight in both directions, rising up into the sky and—the embankment! There were the railroad tracks!

We stopped at the foot of the embankment and I peered up to the top.

"Do we follow along until we hit the road, or do we climb it?" I asked.

"Both," Jack said. "We climb it and then follow along on the other side."

I started up the bank, using my hands to dig in and help pull me up the steep slope. My feet dislodged rocks and cinders and they noisily showered down the slope toward my brother. Looking down I could see that Jack was struggling. He held his injured hand tightly to his chest.

"Let me help you," I called out.

I reached back and grabbed him by his good arm. At that same instant he lost his footing and almost fell over. I struggled to maintain both my grip and my balance and was just barely able to keep us both upright. Together we climbed up. Repeatedly I tripped and felt the cinders and rocks bite into my knees, but I clawed my way forward until we both reached the top.

"Maybe we should rest here," I said, panting.

"Not here . . . too much of a target," Jack replied.

I looked back and suddenly felt very exposed. I could imagine how visible we'd be, our silhouettes standing out on the horizon. Involuntarily I ducked down.

"We'll rest at the bottom," Jack said.

I didn't need any more encouragement. I shuffled over to the other side and dropped down on my bottom. I slid down feet first for a couple of yards. Rocks rained down before me, but at least I was less likely to fall.

"Go down like this," I called back to Jack over my shoulder.

"I'll try."

For a few seconds I'd forgotten about Jack not being able to use his hand and that he needed me.

"Just come down this way. I'll wait for you and help," I offered.

Jack started to pick his way down the slope. His feet slipped out from under him and without thinking he reached back with his hands to cushion the blow, so that he cried out in pain. I scrambled back up and offered a hand. He willingly took it.

As we moved down the slope I thought how strange it was that I was the one helping Jack—and he was letting me. This was so different, something new for us.

Again, Jack let out a yelp. There was no point in asking him if he was all right because I could see, even in the limited light, that his face was distorted with pain.

"It's not much farther," I said reassuringly. "Let me help you down and then we just have to walk. We'll find somebody, or somebody will find us, soon . . . I know they will."

Slowly, together, we slid down the rest of the slope. I could feel my socks and shoes filling up with cinders as we slipped to the very bottom, sending a shower of debris ahead of us.

I'd stood up and was beginning to dust myself off when I became aware that the whole palm of my hand—my good hand—was raw and cut and bleeding. *What will happen next?* I wondered.

Jack was slumped on the ground. "I'm almost positive I know where we are," he said.

"You do?"

"We've been right here before. We came in off the creek from over there," he said, pointing off to a spot invisible in the darkness.

"But isn't that how the Nazis were going to be coming in . . . off the creek?"

"I don't know. Maybe."

"They were asking us all sorts of questions about how we got in," I reminded him.

Suddenly I pictured the darkness around us filled with Nazi agents, all armed, all wanting to kill us. I couldn't imagine anything worse than surviving all we'd survived, getting away and getting this far, only to be recaptured. Recaptured and killed.

"Let's get moving that way," I said, pointing away from the creek. "As fast as we can."

Jack struggled to his feet and we started to move along the base of the railroad embankment.

"You said you know where we are. Are we far from a road?"

"You remember that first night we came here?" he asked.

"That would be hard to forget."

"I think the culvert and that dirt track are just up ahead. But we have to move quickly or it's going to be too late."

We moved to the side, away from the embankment. The ground was much more level and easier to move along quickly. And we were far enough away from the Chief that I wasn't worried about him seeing us.

"There's the track," Jack said.

I strained my eyes to make out a darker ribbon of road cutting through the field. I followed it until it met the embankment and disappeared underneath—the culvert! Still holding onto Jack's good arm, I pulled him along with me. I stumbled forward, not stopping until we broke out onto the dirt track.

"That's where they first stopped us," Jack said, pointing back to the culvert.

"They heard us in the culvert. Maybe that's what we should do this time, go into the culvert and start yelling."

"Let's just head down the road toward headquarters and—"

Suddenly we were hit square in the face by a blinding light, and my hands went up instinctively to shield my eyes.

"Hands in the air!" screamed out a voice.

"Is it . . . is it?"

Jack nodded his head. "It's guards from the camp."

"Thank goodness," I whispered.

"Hands up now or we'll shoot!"

I slowly raised my hands. Beside me, Jack raised one hand right up. The second one, the injured one, was barely at the level of his head.

"It's us!" I called out. "Jack and George! We've got to see the—"

"Shut up!" hissed one of the soldiers as he came toward us. He turned back around to the jeep. "And kill those lights, now!"

Suddenly we were plunged into darkness.

# CHAPTER TWENTY

"ARE YOU TWO GOING to keep coming here until we finally shoot you by accident?" one of the soldiers demanded. His tone was angry, but he was speaking in a voice only slightly louder than a whisper.

"You don't understand—"

"Keep your voice down!" he hissed.

"I'm sorry," I whispered. "It's important that you take us to see the Lieutenant-Colonel right away because—"

"You think we're falling for that again?" he asked.

"What do you mean?"

"Do you know how much trouble those last guards got into for driving you two into the compound?"

"But this is important!" Jack protested.

"Yeah? Well, you can say whatever you want until the cows come home," he said, "there's no way we're driving you to headquarters!"

"You don't have to drive us . . . we can walk," I told him.

"Don't you get it, kid? We're guards. We're supposed to *stop* you from just walking there! That's what guards do!"

"What are you kids even doing out at this time of the night?" the other soldier asked.

"Time . . . that's right, what time is it?" I asked.

"Almost ten-thirty, I think."

"You've got to get us in to see the Lieutenant-Colonel, or Bill or Little Bill. The attacks are supposed to happen at ten-thirty!" I pleaded.

"What are you talking about, kid?"

"The attacks on the munitions plant and the prisoner-of-war camp in Bowmanville," Jack explained.

"And here. They're going to attack here at eleven-thirty," I told him. "They're after somebody . . . somebody important."

"Who's after somebody? Just who is going to launch these attacks you're talking about?"

"German agents. Lots of them," I exclaimed.

"And how would you two know any of this?"

"Mr. Krum told us," I said.

"He's the editor of the paper," Jack added.

"And a German spy," I continued. "He told us after we were tied up, and then they told him to kill us, but he didn't and instead he just pretended to kill us and—"

"That's quite a story," one of the soldiers said, mockingly.

"And they make it really believable. These two are pretty good storytellers."

"Storytellers? What do you mean?" I demanded.

"This is just another test to see if you two can sneak by

security again, isn't it?" one of the soldiers challenged.

"No, it's not a test, honestly."

"Look, boys, even if we did believe you—"

"And we don't, not for a second," the other added.

"Yeah, but even if we did, we can't take you anywhere . . . not to headquarters, not to the gatehouse, no place."

"Why not?" I asked.

"Orders. We're to stay right here at our position."

"But why?"

"They don't tell us why," the first soldier said.

"Yeah, it's on what they call a 'need-to-know basis,'" the second added.

"And apparently we don't need to know much," said the first, and they both laughed.

"But what if something really, really important happened?"

"It doesn't matter if the Prime Minister of the whole darn country walked up to us and told us to drive him to headquarters. We'd tell *him* no, too."

"The Prime Minister . . . he isn't here now, is he?" I was remembering what Mr. Krum had said about them trying to get at somebody important.

"That would be another thing that would be on a need-to-know basis."

"And even if he was," added the second, "and we knew about it, we wouldn't be telling you two."

"So he could be here?" Jack asked.

"Could be."

"Has been before," the second soldier chipped in. "Him and

people even more important."

I struggled to think who could be more important than the Prime Minister. I turned to Jack. He looked back at me desperately. What could we do?

"You're not just going to stay here all night, are you?" I asked.

"Could be. Could be only another five minutes. Depends."

"Depends on what?" Jack asked.

"The radio. They'll call and let us know when we can move."

"The radio!" I gasped. "That's right, you have radios in the jeeps! Can you just call and tell them what we're telling you?"

"No can do. We're under orders to maintain radio silence."

"Radio silence? What does that mean?"

"It means that we can't make calls. We can only listen and wait for them to give us orders."

"Jeez!" exclaimed the second soldier. "We'd better get back to the jeep in case they've been trying to reach us."

"Yeah, come on," the other soldier said, reaching out and grabbing me by the arm. The first soldier grabbed Jack, and he howled in pain.

"What's wrong with you? I hardly laid a glove on you."

"You grabbed my arm . . . my wrist . . . I think it's broken."

"Broken? How'd you do that?"

"When we were trying to get out of the chairs where we were tied by the Germans."

One of the soldiers switched on a flashlight and aimed it at Jack's hand. The wrist was grotesquely swollen!

"That sure does look broken," one of them said.

He ran the flashlight up Jack, passing his ripped shirt, and stopped at his face. Jack tried to shield his eyes with his good hand, but that didn't block the view of the side of his face. It was as badly swollen as his wrist, and it looked like he could barely see out of the one eye.

"It looks like somebody smacked you around!"

"Somebody did!" I snapped. "That's what we've been telling you! After they tied us up, one of the German agents, I think he was the leader, hit Jack when he wouldn't talk!"

"And then George got his hand all cut up getting us out of the ropes."

The light was switched to me. I held out my hands. One was bloody from sliding down the cinder embankment, but the gash on the other glowed even brighter red, and my shirt and pants were painted with blood and mud and marked by rips and tears.

"That looks bad, George," Jack said.

"You both look bad. You need to get to a hospital," one of the soldiers told us.

"We need to speak to the Lieutenant-Colonel!" I insisted.

"And we have orders not to let—"

"Forget the orders!" I snapped. "Do you think we'd do all this to ourselves if we were just trying to make up a story to fool you? We're telling you the truth about everything, and if we can't warn people then they're going to be in big trouble! People will die!"

Neither soldier said anything. The flashlight was turned off.

"You have to believe us," I said.

"I just don't know," one of the soldiers muttered.

"Please."

"Both of you go to the jeep," the first said.

"You're going to drive us?"

"I didn't say that. You two go and sit in the jeep while we talk about this . . . we have to figure this out."

That wasn't the answer I wanted, but it was the closest I'd come to it.

"Come on, George."

Jack and I walked slowly toward the jeep. I turned my head and looked over my shoulder. The two soldiers walked away a few dozen paces and then came to a stop and began talking. In the still night air I could hear their voices above the sound of the gravel crunching under our feet. I strained to hear but could only make out the voices and not the words.

I hopped over the side and into the back of the jeep. Jack climbed in more carefully through the door and then squeezed in between the seats and sat beside me.

"Can you hear what they're saying?" he whispered.

"Not really . . . but it sounds like an argument."

"We don't have time for an argument. We don't have time for anything."

"Look," I said, pointing to the radio that sat between the seats. "Do you know how to use it? Maybe we could call in."

"Even if I did know how to use it, don't you remember what Mr. Krum said?" Jack asked.

"I remember lots of things . . . what do you mean?"

"About him listening in on the radio. If we called, he might hear us."

"I guess you're right."

"Besides, I do know how to use this jeep."

"The jeep?"

"The keys are in the ignition."

"You can't be serious! You're going to steal the jeep?"

"Not steal it. Just borrow it."

"Come on, Jack, let's just wait. Maybe they're going to take us!" I pleaded.

"And if they decide not to? This may be our only chance. Climb behind the wheel."

"Me? Why me?"

"My hand. I can't steer and change gears with just one hand. You've got to do it."

I didn't even know what to say. He wanted me to steal the jeep.

"Hurry up, George."

"I don't even know if I can drive it."

"It's the same as our old tractor. You drove that a thousand times."

"But this isn't our tractor. This is a jeep. An army jeep, and you want me to steal it!"

"Keep your voice down!" he hissed.

"I don't know."

"What's to know? Just turn the keys, throw it into first, pop the clutch and spin the wheel to get us out of here."

"Do you know how much trouble we'll get in?"

"Do you know how much trouble could happen if we don't warn them?" Jack asked.

My point was good. His was better. Reluctantly I rose from the seat and settled in behind the wheel. I stared through the windshield at the two soldiers. They were still arguing, oblivious to what I was doing—and was about to do.

"Turn the key," Jack said.

Just ahead in the darkness I could make out the shapes of the soldiers. I turned the key and the motor roared to life. I pushed it to first, popped the clutch and the jeep jerked forward! Over the roar of the engine I heard the sound of the soldiers yelling and saw their outlines charging toward us! I cranked the wheel and the jeep jumped off the road and roared through the field away from them, bouncing wildly, almost bucking me out of my seat. The only thing holding me in place was my grip on the wheel.

"Turn it, turn it back onto the road!" Jack screamed.

I turned it around and the jeep hit the gravel road and then overshot and bumped off on the other side. Instantly I turned the wheel the other way and first two wheels jumped up onto the gravel, and then the two on the other side!

"Change gears!" Jack screamed.

I pushed down the clutch, and pulled the gear shift back. The jeep groaned and rocked but finally settled into second, and as I pressed down on the pedal it accelerated forward.

"I can't see where I'm going!" I screamed as the wind rushed by.

"The lights! Turn on the lights!"

I fumbled around on the dashboard, searching for the switch. I knew where it was on the tractor, but here I wasn't sure. I pulled a knob and the windshield wipers jumped to life. Desperately I grabbed at another knob and the lights came on! I still wasn't exactly sure where I was going, but at least now I could see. I popped the clutch and threw it into third, accelerating even faster away from the soldiers behind us.

"All positions to the main compound!" screamed a voice over the radio, and I was so startled I almost ran the jeep off the road again.

"Infiltrators by main building! All positions to main compound!" came the voice from the radio.

"They've spotted them!" I screamed.

"Maybe!"

"Of course they have! Who else could it be?"

"Us. It could be us!" he yelled back. "Maybe they think *we're* the infiltrators!"

A rush of fear came over me. If they thought we were the people trying to break into the base, then they'd greet us with a hail of lead. Shoot first, ask questions later. For a split second I eased my foot off the gas pedal—then I plunged it down even farther. Bullets or no bullets, we'd come too far to stop now.

"Look, off to the side!" Jack screamed. "Other vehicles are coming!"

Two sets of headlights were bouncing across the field, coming in our direction.

"We've got to get to the farmhouse before they stop us!" Jack yelled.

*Or before they shoot us,* I thought, but I didn't say anything.

"Faster! Go faster!"

I pushed the pedal right down to the floor. The engine roared and the wind shrieked past my head.

"More company to the right!" Jack yelled.

I glanced over and saw another vehicle charging through the night. This one was barely visible because it had its lights off. It was angling toward us, but we were moving faster and it wasn't going to catch us.

The trail curved sharply and we passed through the orchard—the compound was up ahead. I could just make out the dark shape of the big barn against the sky.

"Blow your horn!" Jack yelled.

"What?"

"Drive with one hand on the horn. We want them to know we're coming. We need the Lieutenant-Colonel to come out!"

"Are you sure?"

"Do it! Just do it!"

I took one hand off the wheel and laid it on the horn. It blared out a warning as we bounced down the road. Our headlights flashed on the barn and I turned the wheel sharply to the right to pass between the buildings and—

"Look out!" Jack screamed.

I jammed on the brakes! Up ahead, trapped in the headlights, was a group of men, all dressed in black. It was Mr. Krum and the German agents! One of them spun around and aimed a rifle right at us! All at once, the muzzle of the gun exploded with a red flare, the windshield of the jeep shattered and I cranked the wheel to the left, crashing through some bushes. And then . . . everything went black.

# CHAPTER TWENTY-ONE

I STARTLED AND SAT bolt upright in bed.

"George! You're all right!" My mother rushed over and threw her arms around me.

"Of course I'm . . . where am I?"

She released me from her grip and I looked around. I was in a bed . . . in a room.

"You're in the hospital. You've been unconscious for almost six hours since the crash."

"The crash . . . that's right . . . we were driving and then we saw them and . . . where's Jack?" I asked desperately. "Is he okay?"

"Jack is fine. He's in the room just across the hall. His wrist and jaw are broken but mainly they just wanted him here for observation."

I let out a big sigh of relief.

"It was you they were worried about. How does your head feel?"

"It feels . . ." I reached up and touched my forehead. It was swollen and painful to the touch.

"You bashed it when you went through the windshield."

"I went through the windshield?" I asked. "I remember the crash and then . . . nothing," I said, shaking my head. "At least everybody's okay."

"Not everybody. I'm so sorry to have to tell you, but Mr. Krum died in the crash."

"He died? Did I hit him?"

"Of course not. He was driving the car."

"No he wasn't, he was in my headlights and I slammed on the brakes and—"

"That's not how it happened. They said you'd be a little confused—the doctor said you had a bad concussion. One of the doctors has been sitting out there every moment since you came in. I'll go and get him. He's such a nice man."

My mother left the room.

What was she talking about, me being in a car with Krum? My head was hurting, but there was no way that I could forget everything and—

"Little Bill!" I exclaimed, as he and another man walked in with my mother.

"I prefer that my patients call me 'Doctor,'" he said with a smile.

"Patients? But . . ."

He was wearing a white lab coat and had a stethoscope around his neck. He did look like a doctor. He winked at me.

"I'm so happy to see that you're up and around." He turned

to my mother. "Would you excuse us while we re-examine our patient?"

"Oh . . . certainly . . . but I was just wondering how he is," my mother said anxiously.

"I'll advise you of everything right after the examination," the other man said.

My mother leaned over and kissed me on the side of the head. "I'll just go over and see your brother. I'll be right across the hall."

She left the room and the door closed behind her.

"Little Bill, what happened?"

"There'll be time to answer all your questions, but first you have to answer this man's questions." He indicated the man beside him.

"Hello, I'm really a doctor," he said. "Do you remember anything?"

"Driving the jeep and seeing those people and . . . waking up here."

"Do you remember the ride to the hospital or talking to me before?" he asked.

"Not really . . . wait . . . did I come here with Bill in the back of a van?"

"Yes, you did," Little Bill answered.

"That's a good sign. Do you know where you are now?"

"In a hospital."

"And do you know your name?"

"Of course," I snorted. What sort of a silly question was that? "I'm George Braun."

"And who was that woman who just left here?" he asked.

"That was my mother."

"Good. Now why don't you two talk while I continue my examination."

"Thanks, Doctor. So, how are you feeling?" Little Bill asked.

"I'm fine . . . I guess . . . but confused."

"That doesn't surprise me at all. You took quite a hit to the head when you crashed the jeep. What questions can I answer to clear things up?"

"I don't know where to start . . . well, maybe with Mr. Krum. Why does my mother think he was killed?"

"He *was* killed," Bill said.

"Did I do it? Did I hit him?"

He shook his head, and I felt a wave of relief wash over me.

"He died in the gunfire. He and two of the other German agents were killed. Two others were wounded, and two were captured uninjured."

"I don't understand. Why did my mother think I was in a car with Mr. Krum?"

"Because that's what we told her," he said. "We had to come up with a story to explain why you and Jack were missing and then injured. It seemed like a logical one, especially in light of the fact that we also had to explain Mr. Krum's death."

"So you just made up a story?"

"It's all part of the spy business. It's almost a contest to see who can come up with the best lies."

The doctor flashed a bright light in my eyes and I recoiled. "Just follow the light," he said.

It hurt my eyes, but I followed the little beam of light as he waved it back and forth.

"Good," he said.

"And those agents, the Germans, they were coming there to get you . . . to kill you!"

Little Bill smiled. "It wasn't me they were after. They were coming to kill Winston Churchill."

"The British Prime Minister was at the camp?" I exclaimed.

"No, but the Germans thought he was."

"Why would they think that?"

"Because that's what we wanted them to believe."

"I don't understand."

"We have been aware of Mr. Krum for a considerable length of time."

"Then why didn't you just arrest him?"

"Ahhh, another espionage trick. We've been feeding him false information for months. We told him what we wanted him to know and he sent back reports that helped us instead of the Nazis."

"Did you know they were coming to the camp?"

He nodded his head. "And that they were launching simultaneous attacks on the munitions plant and the prisoner-of-war camp in Bowmanville. We captured or killed all the German agents." He paused. "It's not difficult when you already know their plans in advance."

"So . . . so when Jack and I were coming to warn you . . ."

"We already knew everything," he said quietly. "We'd been aware of them for two full days prior to the attack. We even tailed them to the abandoned farmhouse."

"The place where they had me and Jack?"

He nodded his head. "If only we'd known you were in there."

"Mr. Krum kidnapped us at gunpoint and we were on the floor of his car and—"

"I know. Jack told us everything."

"We almost died there . . . if it hadn't been for Mr. Krum."

"Jack told us all about that part, too. Poor misguided man, mistaking his loyalty to his homeland for loyalty to the Nazis."

"I'm confused. If you knew about the Nazis, why didn't you come in and capture them earlier? Why did you wait for the attacks?"

"We needed to know if there were other agents involved. We expected that they would get together all their operatives for the attacks. We wanted to clean out the entire rats' nest."

"And were there other agents?"

He shook his head. "None that got away. We caught them all."

"What about Chief Smith?"

Little Bill smiled. "He's of German descent, as are you, but he's as loyal to Canada as anyone. There are very, very few like Krum." He paused and smiled. "You two certainly confused the Chief when you ran away from him out there on the highway. He's agreed to support our cover story about the car accident."

"So you had everything planned right from the start."

"Not everything. We certainly didn't figure on the two of you doing what you did when you came charging into the compound."

"We had to warn—" I stopped myself. They hadn't needed us to warn them about anything. "We almost screwed things up, didn't we?"

"You were an unexpected complication, but you didn't 'screw things up.'"

"You must think that we're a couple of fools," I said, staring down at my bed.

"I was thinking more like a couple of heroes."

"How do you figure that?"

"Let's see. You uncovered a Nazi plot, you escaped capture and, despite injuries, you risked your lives to warn us, somehow again getting by two of my sentries. You were also the first to respond to the alarm and get to the compound to help capture the agents."

"But you didn't need us to warn you," I protested.

"That's not the point. It's what you did and why you did it that makes you both heroes."

I didn't know what to say, but I suddenly felt better . . . a whole lot better.

"So, Doctor, is he going to be okay?" Little Bill asked.

"We'll want him to stay here for a day or so for observation, but he's going to be just fine."

"That's wonderful news, isn't it, George!"

"Yeah, that is good."

"My only regret about this whole matter," Little Bill said, "is that, because of the oath you signed under the Secrecy Act, nobody can know about what you and Jack accomplished. As far as the outside world is concerned, you two were nothing more than survivors of a very bad car accident."

"That's okay. At least we did survive."

"That is a very wise answer."

He came over and reached out his hand to shake mine.

"George, it was an honour to serve with you."

"Um . . . thanks . . . you too," I stuttered.

"Now I think I'd better get your mother and let her know that you're going to be just fine."

He pulled the door open and then paused. "You know, I don't think the Secrecy Act says anything about us telling mothers. We could let her in on some of what happened. What do you think?"

"I think that wouldn't be such a good idea," I said.

He gave me a questioning look.

"If she ever found out what Jack and I have been up to, she'd kill us herself!"

Little Bill burst into laughter. "Not just a hero, but a smart hero. Someday, however, when this is long over, it will be only fitting that people know about what you and your brother did."

"Maybe they should know what everybody did."

He smiled. "Many, many years from now, perhaps. But for now it's enough that *we* know." He turned to leave.

"Wait!" I called out, and he turned back around.

"Will we see you again?"

"Perhaps," he said. "You have to remember that you've been sworn in as operatives. You must remain ready in the event that your services are ever required again."

"We'll be ready . . . just call."

# AUTHOR'S NOTE

ON DECEMBER 6, 1941, situated on 110 hectares in what is now Whitby, Ontario, a "spy school" was created. This camp, while identified under many names by different authorities, came to be known as Camp X. Established under the direction of the head of British Security Co-ordination (BSC), Sir William Stephenson, this facility was created to train Allied agents in sabotage, subversion, intelligence, communications and counter-intelligence. Over the course of the Second World War, hundreds of agents were trained and then sent on the most dangerous of assignments to defeat the Nazis. For the most part, the exploits of these agents remain unknown. But their actions were critical in the final victories of the Allied Forces.

Sir William Stephenson was born and raised in Winnipeg, Manitoba. As head of the BSC, he played a vital role in the entire war effort. He was a quiet, unassuming man in charge of a hidden army of thousands of men and women. He was known as "the Quiet Canadian," "Intrepid" and "Little Bill." The character Little Bill in my novel is a portrayal of Stephenson. He was a truly remarkable individual who was an engineer by training, a successful businessman, a First World War hero, a world amateur lightweight boxing champion and a brilliant espionage agent. One of the men he trained, Ian Fleming, went on to create the character James Bond, and it is rumoured that much of what Fleming created was based on both Stephenson himself and the training he provided to Fleming.

In writing this book I hope to make the reader more aware of Sir William Stephenson and other Canadians who made sacrifices—including the ultimate sacrifice, their lives—to protect our way of life and the freedom we enjoy.

For further information concerning Camp X and William Stephenson, the following sources are highly recommended:

Lynn-Philip Hodgson. *Inside Camp X.* Port Perry, Ontario: Blake Book Distribution, 1999.

H. Montgomery Hyde. *The Quiet Canadian: The Secret Service Story of Sir William Stephenson.* London: Hamish Hamilton, 1962.

William Stevenson, *A Man Called Intrepid: The Secret War.* New York: Lyons Press, 2000.

In addition, the wonderful book *Too Young to Fight,* edited by Priscilla Galloway, is highly recommended in setting the context for characters such as my two protagonists. The book is a collection of short stories, written by many of Canada's finest writers, describing their real experiences during the Second World War.

The characters of Jack and George are fictional creations of the author and are not meant to represent any real people or reflect actual events that took place at Camp X.